MIGRATI

AND OTH

LISA HERNANDEZ

Arte Público Press
Houston, Texas

Migrations and Other Stories is made possible in part from grants from the city of Houston through the Houston Arts Alliance, the University of California at Irvine Chicano/Latino Literary Prize and by the Exemplar Program, a program of Americans for the Arts in Collaboration with the LarsonAllen Public Services Group, funded by the Ford Foundation.

Recovering the past, creating the future

Arte Público Press
University of Houston
452 Cullen Performance Hall
Houston, Texas 77204-2004

Cover design by Giovanni Mora
Cover art courtesy of Judy Baca,
"Triumph of the Hearts" from the World Wall:
A Vision of the Future without Fear, 1990

Hernandez, Lisa
Migrations and Other Stories / Lisa Hernandez.
p. cm.
ISBN 978-155885-499-4
I. Title
PS3608.E7667M54 2007
813′.6—dc22

2006051735
CIP

♾ The paper used in this publication meets the requirements of the American National Standard for Information Sciences—Permanence of Paper for Printed Library Materials, ANSI Z39.48-1984.

7 8 9 0 1 2 3 4 5 6 10 9 8 7 6 5 4 3 2 1

For Louise Sevilla and Kay Murphy

Special thanks to my writers' group, Euphronia Awakuni,
and Eric Wat

And to Scott
Si te quiero es porque sos mi amor, mi cómplice y todo.
M. Benedetti

Contents

Migrations

I spent two weeks in Mexico because I was still burdened by my love for him. Holidays were just too difficult. So on December 24th, I left with a friend, though he really wasn't my friend at the time. Just an acquaintance. In fact, he was my neighbor, Reynaldo, an older man who lived in a converted garage behind my bungalow.

Reynaldo had his own reason for going to Mexico. He hadn't seen his daughter since he left Guadalajara nineteen years ago. Pride had kept him away.

It seemed appropriate to me that I should go to Mexico to forget my past, once and for all, and that he'd go to reconnect to it, and so we bonded through pain like humans do. For this reason, I felt he was my friend, my good friend.

We took separate flights to Guadalajara. He said it was better that way since we weren't lovers, and there was no reason to pretend to be. He would get there first, locate a hotel for us both, and then pick me up at the airport. For two weeks, I could see the sights, while he endeavored to win back his daughter.

I took the red-eye and arrived at four in the morning, Guadalajara time, and realized only after I had claimed my baggage that I had made a mistake and had told him to pick me up at six. For an hour or so, the airport was full of people giving each other holiday hugs and kisses, but after that the airport was completely empty and cold, and I felt very lonely. I began to question whether I had come to Guadalajara for the right reason, but when I saw Reynaldo walking toward me with open arms, I took that as a sign from my guardian angel.

I was sixteen when I took my first plane ride. Since I wasn't part of the Clique, I got stuck sitting next to my history instructor on the flight to Santa Fe. The other girls were having a good time playing charades, but they were making too much noise, and after the second warning, Sister Mary Helen told them that they would not be allowed to leave the retreat house if they continued misbehaving.

I wanted to say something to my history teacher, but I didn't have the nerve since he looked so consumed with his crossword puzzle. His hands were covered in freckles, and he had red hair coming out from under the cuff of his shirt. He had, in fact, red hair all over, and I thought that he was handsome in a weird sort of way.

The week before, the girls had taken a letter out of his desk that he had written to his girlfriend. He wrote that he missed her, that he missed Boston, that he was miserable, that teaching at an all-girls school wasn't all that it seemed, that the pay sucked, and that, all jokes aside, being the only male among a horde of pubescent women was mortifying. Copies were made of the letter and distributed to all the girls. Those in the Clique hadn't decided what exactly they were going to do to Mr. Keeley to mortify him some more.

I waited for my two suitcases at the baggage claim. One was a solid black Samsonite case with a yellow ribbon. The other was a beat-up, small blue valise that had a rope tied around it. I had argued helplessly with my mother to leave it, but my mother insisted that the notice that Sister Mary

Helen sent home said that the girls would need extra food since the retreat house only provided the essentials. I told my mother that it was too much food and that the Clique wouldn't like it anyway, but my mother said that white people loved tortillas, that her *frijoles* were the best, and not to worry so much about what the other girls thought of me. When the valise passed by on the conveyer belt, I let it pass because Mr. Keeley was right next to me, but when all the suitcases started disappearing, it only became more prominent. "Let's go, let's go, let's go," he kept yelling, so I grabbed the valise and ran behind him.

As I was running, the rope busted and the valise flew open. Plastic bags full of rice and beans fell out and Gerbers bottles full of salsa splattered on the floor. A thick, five-dozen tortilla bag rolled by Mr. Keeley's feet.

Guadalajara was cold. The hotel room smelled of Pine-Sol, and since I hated the smell, I opened the window, but the draft was unbearable. The hotel room wasn't in the center of the city, and it was going to be a problem getting around. The busboy insisted that Guadalajara had great public transportation, that the taxis were very reliable, and that he could, in fact, refer a taxi driver if I needed one. I smirked, but gave him a nice tip anyway. He was just trying to earn a buck like everybody else, I thought.

I decided to walk down the street and find out what was nearby while I waited for Reynaldo to return from his old neighborhood. He had gone there to confirm his daughter's address. I wanted to see the murals of Orozco, visit the Mercado and the Lago de Chapala, and maybe take a day trip to Tequila and light a candle in the Basilica. At the corner, I saw a street market full of food vendors with steaming pots of *caldos* and *cocidos*. When I sat down to expand my list of things to see and eat a bowl of menudo, I saw Reynaldo crossing the street.

His eyes were red and a little puffy. The collar of his jacket was pulled up, and he shrugged when he saw me as if the cold was too much for him. He wiped his nose with his handkerchief.

"I fucking hate this city," he said as he sat down. "It's a shit town and I'm happy I left it when I did."

"Why?"

"It's too fucking cold."

"It's pretty cold," I replied. I waited for him to explain, but he said nothing. "So what happened?"

"Not only did the bitch completely blow me off, she threw me out of the pharmacy. She told me it would be a cold day in hell before she'd let me meet my grandchildren, that she had told them I was dead, anyway, and as far as she was concerned I was. Can you fucking believe that?"

I took in the intense smell of the steaming bowl of menudo in front of me. "What are you going to do now?"

"I don't know," he said, defeated.

I struggled to chew the large pieces of tripe. The soup was extremely hot and so spicy it grabbed at my throat and sent tears to my eyes.

"How's the menudo?" Reynaldo asked.

"Pretty good," I replied. "Have some." I pushed the bowl toward him.

He raised his hand. "Listen, let's go to Guanajuato. It's a better town, more history, cleaner, nicer people. Things aren't so goddamn far apart."

"Tonight?"

"Now. The bus station is only five minutes away."

By nine that night it was raining hard, and we were on a bus to Guanajuato. Reynaldo fell asleep the moment he sat in his seat. His hand was still clutching the white handkerchief. I was sorry that the day had gone so terribly for him, and I felt like placing my hand on his, but I resisted the feeling because it would only complicate things, and anyway, the fact that I was there next to him on this third-rate bus in the middle of nowhere in the fucking cold pretty much said it all.

As soon as we left the city, everyone on the bus dropped their curtains and got ready to watch a Van Damme movie. It was some ridiculous, plotless adventure flick that I was compelled to watch because the TV monitor was right in front of me. A boy sitting behind me was practicing his Van Damme kicks right up my back. I thought of turning around and smacking him hard on the forehead and knocking him out for the night, but instead I closed my eyes, shut out all noise, and thought of him.

It had been sixteen months since I last saw him. One fight after another—the jealousies, the money problems (I didn't have any, and he did), the age difference—ended in my packing my stuff into my Volkswagen and leaving without a place to go. I spent two nights at a cheap hotel on Sunset before I found the bungalow.

I remembered one morning when we were washing dishes together and he casually said that all immigrants who crossed the border illegally were criminals, knowing full well that my parents were immigrants who had crossed the border illegally. I swore that I'd never forgive him for saying that, for having such a mean streak, for being such an utter asshole, but I did the moment he apologized. Later that day, he brought me sunflowers and two books—anthologies on Chicano literature. As I paged through the books, I told him that when I was a kid I couldn't defend myself and that I thought that as I grew older it would be easier, but that he always made me feel helpless.

That night we made love, and I felt as though my body had risen above the bed. He said that he'd felt the same, but I didn't believe him until he was able to describe the same feeling of suspension, the lightness, the exact moment when it happened. Why I felt that that one time, I wasn't sure. Maybe because I knew it was over, that it was the beginning of the end.

It was three in the morning when we arrived in Guanajuato. There was some festival going on and all the hotel rooms were booked. Reynaldo insisted that the tourist agents at the bus depot find us a room. He hugged me tight, apologized a hundred times, and said that if we found even one room he'd sleep on the floor, but after calling every hotel in the vicinity, we finally gave up.

We slept in the hard, orange depot seats for two hours, but it was unbearable, so we left Guanajuato and went to Leon, which was about an hour away. Everyone assured us that we could find a room there.

I wasn't going to get into the pool anyway, I thought, when Mr. Keeley knocked on my door and requested that I follow him to the lounge. Some girls were watching *Breakfast at Tiffany*'s with Sister Mary Helen, who stood up dramatically as soon as she saw me and explained that I needed to pack immediately and catch the next flight out, that my grandmother was seriously ill, that my family would meet me at the airport, and that I should remember that the grace of God was always with me. Mr. Keeley drove me to the airport in the campus ministry van without saying a word.

When we got to the airport, he took my suitcase, walked me to the gate, and then gave me a tight hug. I felt my face flush. No man outside my family had ever hugged me that tight before.

"I'll miss you," I said without thinking.

"Me, too," he smiled. Mr. Keeley was a good man.

While in line at the gate, I turned back to see if he was still there. He waved to me. I stared into his kind eyes, and it made me want to cry.

When I got to Los Angeles my father and sister were waiting for me at the gate. I asked about my grandmother. She was very ill. They didn't know any more than that.

My grandmother lived alone in a ranch near Lerdo. It was a really small town in northern Mexico, and there was only one flight out twice a week. My mother, two sisters, and my uncle had taken a flight out that morning. The rest had waited for me to come home, so we could drive there. The drive was twenty-three hours. We would arrive ten hours before the second flight to Lerdo if we drove nonstop. Five people—my sister, two cousins, my father, and me—would drive there in my sister's Cherokee.

As soon as we started driving south on the 405 freeway, I remembered why I hadn't gotten in the pool. I felt the moisture of my period starting.

"Can we go back home?" I asked. "I forgot something." I needed sanitary napkins and fuller fitting underwear.

"What did you forget?" my father asked.

"Clothes and some other stuff," I replied.

"What is wrong with you?" my sister yelled at me. "Didn't you hear that grandmother is really sick? We're eating in the car and stopping only to get gas. And you better use the restroom then."

"Can we stop at the next gas station?" I insisted.

My sister threw up her hand, and my father adjusted the rearview mirror to look at me. I could feel the weight of his eyes observing me. "I'll stop as soon as I see something," he said.

Because Leon is the leather capital of Mexico, Reynaldo insisted that I purchase a leather jacket or a pair of boots. We shopped all morning until we found a camel-colored jacket that I liked very much. He paid for it without asking my permission, insisting that it was the cost of spending those horrible hours at the bus depot.

We left at noon and headed for Guanajuato, and there we spent the rest of the day visiting the mummy museum, a silver mine, and a monastery with a torture chamber in the basement that had been used during the Inquisition. Encased in glass was a metal chastity belt with protruding, jagged metal spikes down the front in the shape of a vagina. Reynaldo said that every woman has one of these belts but that she won't show it until a man has fallen in love with her. He said, "And once he goes in, he'll never be able to get out again." I rolled my eyes and asked him to stand by the encasement so I could take his picture. He faked a look of horror for the camera.

We took a taxi to a church that was, according to the taxi driver, the great Basilica of Guanajuato, but we felt little inspiration. The inspiration came later that night from a bottle of *mezcal* we drank in his hotel room.

"She was so cute when she was a baby," he said. "She had big, rosy cheeks and long, curly hair, and her nose was petite. Look at my nose. It's not a bad nose, is it?"

"Long and thin. It's a nice nose," I agreed.

"Well now she's fat. And she cropped her hair. And that nose looks like a snout. Identical. Identical. Identical. A big snout!"

"There isn't any resemblance of when she was a baby?"

"None. Absolutely none. I want my money back," he said, smiling. He became silent, and I could see his sadness.

"Do you regret leaving?"

"Not really," he said. "Sometimes."

"Then why did you leave?"

"To work. Like everybody else. I left home to find work in Los Angeles I was twenty-seven, had no money, and I wanted to join my uncle's truck driving business, but I couldn't unless I had my own truck. So I left my wife and kid with the intention of working to save up for the truck, but six months turned into one year, and that turned into another year. And I felt lonely.

"I rented a room for ten bucks a week in one of those big Victorian homes just beyond the bridge that crosses into East Los Angeles. There was a cantina across the street that I'd go to. And there I saw the most beautiful woman I had ever seen in my life and fell immediately in love with her. Her name was Lucía, and she was a waitress—mind you, a waitress in a Mexican cantina—but I didn't care. I picked her up every night after work and ravaged her in my rented room, and one week turned into a year, and that turned into ten, and those were the happiest years of my life. That woman was the love of my life.

"Then one day, I came home from work, and she was gone. No note, no warning. She was just gone."

When we got to Lerdo, we found my aunt's house empty, so we drove directly to my grandmother's house, which took another hour and a half—not because it was far but because there wasn't a road. My father had to drive slowly over the potholes and through a narrow dirt road between a field and a canal. My sister wanted to go directly to the hospital, but my father said there were three hospitals in Lerdo and that our grandmother could be at any of the three.

Once we finally got to the little farmhouse, I saw several cars parked next to the stable door. Inside, my grandmother's coffin had been placed awkwardly on a table that had been moved from the kitchen to the bedroom. As we walked in, people screamed. My mother fell to her knees in front of us. Cousins rushed to lift her from the floor. My father pushed himself back against the wall and slipped into a haunch. His hand covered his face.

Someone ordered my cousin José to feed the animals, since they hadn't been fed in days, my cousin Salvador to contact our distant relatives in Colima, and my cousin Gustavo to find a priest. I thought it was my mother ordering people around. In fact, I was quite sure that it was my mother ordering people around in between wails. The wails seemed distant, though, as I approached the coffin.

My grandmother looked as though she were sleeping, as though she would wake any minute and tell me that I had a little angel inside my right ear and a little devil in the left ear. From the time I could remember, my grandmother had told me this, and so I equated good and bad with right and left. I found it amusing, though, that we were both very left-handed.

Every time my grandmother told me about my rights and lefts, she would add that I should always try to listen to the little angel in my right ear. But then she'd pause, smile mischievously, and blurt out a dramatic "but": two husbands, a revolution, numerous droughts, and much other heartache later, she understood how necessary it was to listen to the little devil in the left ear, particularly, ahem, when it came to men, which would segue into an outrageous sexual story that almost always included promiscuous priests, donkeys with very large penises, and women with very hairy bushes. My grandmother's laughter was intense, with a contagious hissing that, if it lasted too long, would send her running to the bathroom.

He didn't like the idea of going to see the monarchs because it was two hours away from Guanajuato, but I told him that seeing so many beautiful butterflies all at once would really be special, wouldn't it? He rolled his eyes but bought the tour tickets anyway.

We took a shuttle bus that had a big orange-and-black monarch painted on it. It was a long, bumpy, boring ride, and when we finally got there, several of the townspeople explained to us that the monarchs had died in thunderstorms that had swept the area for weeks. Still, they said, it was a sight to see. The ground was covered with dead monarchs, and the smell, they insisted, was tolerable. Reynaldo said that we should demand a refund, that we weren't spending an entire day and thirty dollars to see dead insects, but I calmed him down and convinced him to go on the tour anyway.

The hike was tiring but the smell was, in fact, tolerable. Not anything I could really place, except maybe a bit musty. A pale yellow-orange carpet extended hundreds of feet, and I was afraid to walk on it for fear of stepping on the monarchs, but it was inevitable.

We walked a bit more, then stopped to sit on a huge rock. That's when I saw two big, beautiful monarchs flying together just above the ground. They were mating, perhaps, as they'd rise, fall, and rise again. The fall was much more dramatic than the rise. The weight of both of them was too much.

When we got back, we were able to take a long walk through the town because it wasn't quite as cold as the day before. I walked ahead of Reynaldo trying to remember signs so we'd be able to find our way back, but I got tired and eventually tucked my arm inside his. It was the day before New Year's Eve. The plaza was full of strolling couples, of women selling *champurrado* and tamales, and of vendors selling monarch mementos.

We sat at a restaurant in the plaza. Reynaldo warned me not to order *mariscos*, that we were nowhere near water, and that the *mariscos* would not be fresh, but I ordered a shrimp cocktail anyway and had several Coronas with it. He ordered soup but didn't like it, and so he ordered *chicharrones*. I warned him that eating pork was dangerous, that the place didn't look that clean, but he ate it anyway and ordered three *cubitas* after that. I muttered that pork and brandy could really make him ill. He smiled at me and said that he was having a great time, that his stomach was made of steel, and asked me if vacation partners should always be this difficult.

The temperature dropped a lot that night, and the hotel room was freezing. I searched the room for the heater switch, and when I couldn't find it, I went to Reynaldo's room to ask him to help me with it, but he told me the room didn't have a heater. I was really upset and my face showed it because Reynaldo went downstairs and argued with the hotel clerk. I heard him ask for more blankets, but when I saw him walk up again empty-handed, I thought I was going to cry. I hated, absolutely hated, being cold. He hugged me tight for a long while.

When he let go, I walked into his room and got into his bed. He went and got my blanket, folded it in two, and threw it over me. A minute or so passed before he got into bed with me. Another minute or so passed before he turned off the light. Still another minute or so passed before he kissed me. His manner was smooth and intuitive. I had never been with a man so much older than me, but making love made me completely forget how cold I was, and I guess I fell asleep in his arms.

The men were drunk outside the house. Several old men—my great-uncles and distant cousins—wept aloud as they remembered their childhoods. Occasionally, the wails from inside the house would increase as the women took turns saying the rosary. I knew I should have been inside with the women, but I couldn't stand seeing the coffin, and I wanted to be with my father, who sat outside with the rest of the men.

My great-uncle, a very old man with a ten-gallon hat and pointed boots that he could barely walk in, put his hand on his cane as he wept softly. He said he wasn't crying for his sister but for himself. She was with our heavenly father, but he was left on this earth to suffer her loss. He said that if old men cry so much, it's only because they finally understand life. But he would bear the loneliness with goodwill toward God. After all, *Nuestro Padre Dios* had not given him his sister, he had only lent her to him. And it was right and appropriate that whatever was lent be returned.

And then he leaned on his cane and addressed my father. He spoke louder, perhaps because he wanted all the other men to hear him. He said that although up to that point it had been unspoken, he loved my father like a son, that he admired how focused and responsible he had been all his life, and that the family was proud of him.

My father stared into the night sky. I felt bad for him because I knew how much he wanted to cry, but couldn't, so I put my head on his lap and thought tender thoughts—like how much I loved him, that I knew how much he loved my grandmother, and that this was all very sad and it was okay to cry. I wanted these thoughts to reach his heart and console him, but I dozed off.

My father shook my shoulders an hour or so later. He was still sitting stiffly in his chair. It was three or four in the morning. I told him that I wanted to bathe, but he said there wasn't enough time or water for that. The day's ration of water had been used and there was no one to heat it. But it was the third day of my menstruation, and I felt a desperate need to bathe. Every summer since I could remember, my grandmother had run a bath for me because there was no indoor plumbing, and she had to heat the water over the adobe fire pit that was near the stable.

I found a large washbasin in the garden and dragged it beyond the horse stable to the back room of the house, which had at one time been my mother's bedroom but was now empty except for a chicken that flew in and out of the large hole in the wall that served as a window. I looked for a corner away from the door and placed a chair there. Then I went to my grandmother's kitchen and found the lantern that was kept on a wood plank near the stove. I lit the lantern and searched the room. My mother's umbilical cord was buried in that room as were my sisters'. Mine would have been buried there too had I not been born in Los Angeles.

I placed my soap and towel on the chair and stood in the ice-cold water that had been left in the reserve tank. As I wet the sponge with soap and water, I wondered whether my grandmother was with the little angel or the little devil, and whether she got to choose, and if God were a man, ahem, whether she'd chosen the devil. A terrifying thought entered my mind. I would never know if my grandmother was safe or happy—or laughing as she usually was in life. My arms trembled as I passed the sponge over them. I pulled the pail of cold water near me, dipped a bowl into it, and dropped it over my head. For a moment, I thought I might lose consciousness.

When I got back to the main bedroom, I found the black dress that my sister had given me to wear. It was matronly and too big, and I didn't have any shoes but my penny loafers. I knew I looked ridiculous, but I told myself it didn't matter.

In the patio, I began to feed the parakeets in little wooden cages hanging against the wall. My grandmother loved birds, and these little ones were her favorites. I wondered if my mother would allow me to release the parakeets before we returned to Los Angeles. I turned and stared at the long, needle-like beak of the blue jay in the pomegranate tree. The parakeets wouldn't last a week. Or would they?

From the patio, I heard my mother arguing with my uncle. She wanted my grandmother buried next to my grandfather, but he said that it couldn't be done because there were too many rocks there.

"Dig it anyway," she said.

"We already tried, but we hit granite. We can't break it with the shovels that we have," he said.

"Borrow machinery from Padilla," my mother said.

"There's no time for that," he responded.

"How deep is the hole?" she asked.

"It's too shallow!" he yelled. "Stop insisting! We still have the bigger problem of finding a priest."

"I could care less about the priest. How can you possibly consider burying our mother anywhere but next to him."

"At three this afternoon we are going to bury our mother, with or without a priest, and next to or not next to our father, and that's that!" my uncle yelled as he walked out of my grandmother's kitchen. I heard plates crash and my mother shout out my grandmother's name, imploring her guidance during this most difficult of times.

The next five hours went by very quickly. My sisters arrived from the relatives' homes where they were staying. My aunts, uncles, and godparents arrived also with about a hundred or so cousins. Then the townspeople started arriving. My uncle parked his truck in front of the house, and he and my other uncles, my father, and my eldest cousins went in to close the coffin, which was made of rough wood and had no handles. The men had to heave it onto their shoulders and carefully slide it into the truck bed. Everyone would walk the two miles to the cemetery.

The truck produced so much dust that everyone in the procession had to place their handkerchiefs or hands over their mouths. More townspeople joined the procession as the truck passed in front of their homes. Women wept loudly, but no one as loudly as my mother, who collapsed twice on the way. My cousins, two strong men twice her size, struggled to keep her up.

When we got to the cemetery, I saw two holes: a shallow one next to my grandfather's grave and the one where they would bury my grandmother about twenty feet from it. When the old men began to speak, the crowd pushed forward, and I lost sight of my mother and sisters.

I stood near the shallow hole and stared at the rocks. They had indentations on them, probably from the shovels trying to penetrate the earth, but it was impenetrable, as impenetrable as my grandmother's being gone, as the uncertainty of an afterlife, as the existence of a God. I realized that there were some truths that could not be broken down.

I looked for my father who was away from the crowd, staring up at the sky, lost in his thoughts. I wondered if he was reading the clouds for meaning. I looked up with him, and I told myself that the clouds were calling my grandmother's spirit. They were finding a place for her somewhere in the nebulousness of the sky.

Reynaldo left the hotel room early, and when I awoke and saw that he wasn't there, I took a deep breath and looked quickly around the room to see if I saw his stuff. I saw a note on the pillow that he would wait for me in the hotel restaurant.

When I arrived at the table, I noticed that he had already eaten. He looked tired, and he hadn't shaved. He reached his hand across the table and over mine and said that tomorrow was New Year's Day and that he had to return to Guadalajara, if only one last time. I told him that it was dangerous to travel on New Year's Eve. Everyone got drunk and fired off guns. He looked unimpressed.

I told him the story of when my family traveled by bus to Mexico City via the dangerous Sierra Madre mountains on New Year's Day, how the bus driver was drunk, and how he took the winding, narrow road without turning on and off his lights like he was supposed to do and nearly killed my family and all the other passengers by smashing into a semi full of lumber. He continued to stare at me unimpressed and told me not to be difficult, and he said it in a tone that I had never heard before in him. Only yesterday he had found my insistence charming. Sex brought out a different tone in him, and I didn't like it.

The bus ride back to Guadalajara was uneventful. We arrived in the early hours of the morning and installed ourselves in a hotel not too far from the Mercado. He left as soon as we got there to look for his daughter.

Just outside the hotel, some street merchants from Chiapas were laying out textiles in bold greens and reds, but the jolting colors only mildly interested me. I went to see the murals of Orozco at a gallery near the Mercado Benito Juarez. The tour guide was a young, unattractive man, who although knowledgeable was also very arrogant. But I didn't care too much because the murals were consuming, and I thought only about them for the afternoon.

When I got out, I took a taxi to Tonala and shopped for a couple of hours. I bought Reynaldo a T-shirt that read, "I visited Guadalajara and survived." It had a large tequila bottle on it. When I got back to the hotel room, he was already there, slumped on the bed, waiting for me. He asked me if I would accompany him, that his daughter Camelia had agreed to let him meet his grandchildren. She would have said no again, but her husband had insisted.

Although I had apprehensions about going, I said yes without hesitating, and I met him an hour later in the lobby.

Camelia's *pozole* was delicious, and the conversation was light and mostly between the men. I helped Camelia heat tortillas in the kitchen. She said little to me, and she stared at my hair, at my hands, and at my neck. The intensity of her stare made me feel ashamed. I was at least five years younger. I wondered if having slept once with Reynaldo qualified me as being his lover. I didn't want to be the lover of this woman's father.

Neither Reynaldo nor Camelia drank, but Camelia's husband—a pharmacist—nearly drank a six-pack of Tecate by himself. I drank a beer and felt like having at least another to calm my nerves, but the pharmacist had drunk them all.

We talked about the cold weather in Guadalajara, which segued into the California weather, which segued into a lengthy description of Disneyland. The four children really enjoyed Reynaldo's description of the nighttime parades. The eldest was a twelve-year-old boy and the youngest was a three-year-old girl. They were beautiful, big-eyed like their father, and very polite.

Reynaldo fell immediately in love with his granddaughter. He played with her hair, gave her a piggyback ride, tickled her. Her name was Eunice, and she seemed quite comfortable being the center of attention. He told her that he was going to bring her a big doll—bigger than her—two times bigger than her—from Los Angeles.

The twelve-year-old, a quiet boy with glasses, would start each question in Spanish with, "Would you permit me to ask . . . ?" He asked me about Hollywood, the Rose Parade, Universal Studios, and finally about Disneyland. The other two ten-year-old boys—identical twins—sat next to me also as I went into a lengthy description of the pirates in Pirates of the Caribbean. I was about to get into a description of Space Mountain when Camelia blurted out, "You abandoned me! Why did you abandon me? You said I would always be your little girl and you abandoned me!"

Everyone froze as she cried hysterically. I noticed the eyes of the twelve-year-old getting watery.

Reynaldo nearly dropped the little girl. He looked dumbfounded. Eunice frowned and started patting his chest.

He said quietly, "I left, but I never abandoned you."

"For nineteen years!" Camelia screamed. "Who was here for my first communion, for my wedding? Who walked me down the aisle? Who was here when my first child was born? When Luis lost his job and we lost the house? Who was here? You weren't. You abandoned me! You coward! You're nothing but an irresponsible coward!"

Camelia got up and started pacing. Eunice began to scream. The older boy picked Eunice up and sat her on his lap. He kissed his sister on the forehead and began to bounce her on his knee.

The pharmacist stood up and went over to hug his wife. He pulled up her chin and said, "Your father is a guest in our home, what's in the past is in the past, right now you need to calm down."

Camelia looked at her husband intently, as if he were the only person in the room, as if he were transmitting something to her through his eyes, and it seemed to calm her. The couple's unspoken intimacy made me feel jealous. Who was this pharmacist who could calm his wife so quickly in a moment of crisis?

Then Reynaldo blurted out, "Let me ask you this. Who paid for your communion dress, and who paid for the hall when you got married? How dare you say I abandoned you! Who the hell paid your way through school? Who cashed his check every month and went directly to the post office to send money home? Who the hell do you think you are to tell me that?" His voice broke when he said those last words, and he gasped as though he were choking.

The pharmacist got up and searched in the cabinet for his bottle of tequila. He took a big slug, sent the boys to play ball outside, and took his little girl from his son. He shook his head as if to say a thousand pardons and poured Reynaldo a drink.

He spoke softly. "It must be painful . . . for the two of you. So many years. But here you are. It's like a second chance. God has blessed you." He reached his hand out to Camelia who was still pacing.

When she took his hand, he said to her, "Sit down and talk to your father. He will always be your father."

Camelia's face fell into her hands, and she started weeping. There was a long, awkward silence before she got up and said she was going to heat water for coffee. The pharmacist started talking about his pharmacy to his father-in-law, how it had taken so much work to be able to purchase it, how it was now quite successful, and that perhaps in a couple of years he would open another one in the center of town to secure a future for his sons and, of course, for little Eunice.

Camelia waited in the kitchen until the water boiled, and she rinsed the coffee cups she had in her china case. When the coffee was prepared, she told the kids to come back, and the group started talking about Eunice's baptism party. Camelia took out pictures and showed them to her father. A tear would roll down her cheek every now and then. The children took out more shoeboxes full of pictures and showed Reynaldo their first Holy Communion photos. Then they started showing him wedding pictures. The pharmacist boasted about his weight and good hair back then, and everyone made fun of his ruffled seventies shirt and pastel blue suit.

It was two in the morning when I told them that I was really tired and needed to sleep. The pharmacist insisted I share the twin bed with Eunice. Camelia lent me pajamas.

When I walked down the stairs early the next morning, I found the pharmacist asleep on the sofa. He had fallen asleep in his clothes. The poor man hadn't even taken off his shoes. I told him that I was going to the hotel to shower and change. He offered me their shower, but I politely said I needed a change of clothes, so he drove me to the hotel.

At the hotel, I showered, packed, and turned in my key. From the lobby, I called Reynaldo. He was eating breakfast with the children. I told him I had decided to leave. He asked me to stay, that we hadn't toured Guadalajara together yet, and that he wanted to invite everyone to eat dinner at one of the fancy restaurants in the plaza.

I told him I'd see him in Los Angeles He said he felt bad that I was cutting my trip short. But I told him I wasn't going home yet.

I reminded him that while he had reconnected to his past, I had not forgotten mine. There was still some forgetting to do. Besides, he was right: Guadalajara was too spread out, too much like Los Angeles, and Guanajuato *was* prettier. I was going back there.

I'd revisit the monastery and that church on the hill. I would follow those remaining butterflies a little while longer.

The Neighbor

Sarita was seventy-nine years old. She never had a child but she had sixteen songs. Beautiful, sad ones that she sang in Guadalajara after her first true love died. They were hers only because she gave them life, the kind of depth she knew she had. But those days were long gone. She had two husbands after that. And they too had died. "*¡La tragedia la sigue!*" her neighbors would say. Still, five years ago, you could hear her humming her favorites in the backyard with her canary. Then it died too, and she stopped humming altogether.

It was Tuesday, a warm June night, and Sarita was in bed with the remote in her hand flipping the Spanish channels when the news blared. Lola Beltrán, the great Mexican singer, had died. Latin America was in mourning. She turned the TV off. "*¡Dios mío, qué pena!*" she said as she patted her pillow and rolled over. "Lola used to make me want to sing."

Then she heard screams from next door. Piercing screams. It was her neighbor Matilde and her boyfriend Gustavo. Sarita had heard them making love earlier. Matilde had moaned all afternoon. Sarita pulled the blanket off and stood on her bed to close the window. She heard Gustavo yell, "You bitch whore, why don't I just kill you?" Matilde pleaded, "Please, Gustavo, please!"

The next day, Sarita looked out the kitchen window and saw Matilde crying on her patio. Sarita shook her head as she sliced the flan carefully, whip-creamed the top, and then walked down her driveway and over to Matilde's house. The door was open, so Sarita walked through the house to the patio and placed the flan on the wicker table. As soon as Matilde saw Sarita, she sobbed, "He says that he's going to leave me. That it's over. That he hates me!"

"Well, little girl, then that means he must hate you. Believe a man when he says he hates you."

Matilde was not a little girl. She was a thirty-five-year-old woman and Sarita knew it, but she couldn't stand Matilde. She was such a *chillona*. Still, Sarita had known her all her life, and it was more habit than affection that made her keep an eye out for Matilde, that and the fact that Matilde's mother, Reina, had been Sarita's closest friend and *comadre*.

"He can't hate me. You don't understand. He must have another woman. I found a video store receipt in his pocket, and it has his address listed in South Central. Come with me?"

"No."

"Please, Sarita. I'll be able to leave him if I know there's another woman."

"No."

"You don't understand. If I don't go, I'll go out of my mind! I'll hurt myself! I don't know what I'll do! I can't drive by myself. Please, Sarita, please come with me!"

Sarita got into Reina's beat-up Grand Marquis. The car was immaculate when Reina was alive. Sarita remembered how the family hovered over the dying Reina on the sofa, crying, fighting for her attention. Reina shouted at her sisters, "No, I want Sarita to take me to the restroom." And there on the toilet seat, while Reina struggled to pee, she told Sarita, "I'm going to die. Please take care of my little girl for me."

Sarita snapped at Matilde, "*Niña*, drive slower! Why are you in such a hurry to find out what you already know?"

They drove past railroad tracks, boarded-up houses, and teenagers clustered in front of apartment buildings. Matilde slowed down and then stopped in front of a huge apartment complex, new and already falling apart.

Matilde said, "This is it."

She turned into the long drive that led to about a hundred carports. "There's his car!" she panted. She stopped the car and reached for the door handle.

"Matilde, where are you going? Can't you see? He has a lover."

"But why?" Matilde sobbed.

"What does it matter?"

"If I see her, I'll stop seeing him. I have to," Matilde said as she walked toward the apartment.

Sarita slid over into the driver's seat and drove behind her. Matilde looked back and waved her hand to stay back, but Sarita started honking loud—five, ten, fifteen times. A hand pulled back the curtains in the apartment above the carport but no one opened the door. When Matilde saw the hand, she ran up the stairs and knocked. No one answered. She knocked again and then placed her cheek against the door and started sobbing hysterically. With her cheek still against the door, she slid into a squat.

"*Pendeja,*" muttered Sarita as she watched Matilde from the car. Sarita had had three husbands and innumerable lovers and not once had she begged like Matilde.

"*Pinche pendeja*," she repeated. "A man should come to you—should beg you!" Sarita jerked the car back and then drove out slowly. When Matilde saw the car leaving, she ran down the stairs. Sarita waited at the end of the driveway.

Sarita stood in front of the altar she had made for Reina years ago for All Souls Day. It was on the kitchen windowsill and had two votive candles (lilac, because that was Sarita's favorite), a miniature bottle of El Venado tequila (every birthday they'd get drunk together), and a barrette made of mother-of-earth pearls that Sarita had given to Reina for her fiftieth birthday and had taken back after she died.

The barrette was a gift from her first husband when she was still Sarita, La Perla de México, her stage name. Sarita looked at the Polaroid of Reina and herself. They were cheek to cheek, hands on hips, showing off for the camera. Sarita wasn't a woman of faith and Reina knew it, but she always thought the best of her. Sarita sighed as she looked at the picture.

"Really, Reina, it's a shame you died. Your daughter needs you so much. She's such an idiot. You raised her weak. You protected her too much! Why didn't you give her any of you? Today I did two things for you. Just so you know, this makes up for the time I flirted with your brother and for not paying you back when you lent me money for a new refrigerator."

Then the phone rang. It was Matilde. "Sarita, I can't get out of bed."

"Why not?" Sarita asked.

"I don't know how to explain . . . I just can't get out of bed."

"Why?"

"He slapped me and pushed me and I fell."

"Are you alone?"

"Yes."

"Okay, *niña*." Sarita hung up, put her slippers on, and walked over.

The room was a mess. Clothes on the floor, plates of food, glasses and cups everywhere. Matilde's eyes were puffy, her face pale. She was in a white nightie.

"I'm bleeding," Matilde said softly. "I'm bleeding and I'm pregnant," she repeated. "I want this baby so much." She began to sob.

Sarita knew the feeling. At her age, she had wanted a child too. Maybe it was the one thing that she missed out on in her life. Of course, with a child as stupid as Matilde, it was hard to say.

Matilde moaned, "Maybe I should go to the doctor?"

"Maybe? Maybe you should stay here and bleed to death? What do you think?" Sarita said as she picked up clothes from the floor.

"Will you take me, Sarita?"

"Where are the keys?" Sarita said reluctantly as she looked up at the ceiling. "This one is for the time I flirted with your cousin Alfredo and made him have that terrible fight with Amparo the night of your anniversary party."

Matilde had a miscarriage, and because her uterus collapsed, she had to have a hysterectomy. In the hospital room, Matilde asked Sarita to hold her hand while they prayed for the dead baby.

As they said the rosary, Sarita began to think of Salvador, her second husband, how when he was dying in a hospital bed he had asked her to hold his hand, too. "Forgive me for leaving you so early," he had whispered into her ear and then brought her close and kissed her forehead. Sometimes when she slept, usually in the early morning hours, Sarita could feel the brush of his breath on her ear. That's how she knew his spirit had spent the night with her. But this was more than Sarita wanted to remember, so she left Matilde and sat in the waiting room until Gustavo arrived. There, the two exchanged dirty looks, and then Sarita went home.

And that was the end of that. Weeks passed and no noise came from the house next door. Sarita would see Matilde scurry in and out of the house taking Gustavo's clothes to the cleaners. Sarita thought Matilde was avoiding her, so she called and left a message that she planned to stop by and pick the avocado and lemon trees. "Your mother would never have let them rot this way," Sarita said.

Later that day, Matilde called to tell her that Gustavo had asked to marry her. She said that everything was fine, that she was very busy, but she was happy and she'd drop a basket of lemons and avocados by as soon as she had a chance.

Sarita looked at Reina's altar and said softly, "That girl puts you to shame. If she wants to be with that idiot, then that's her problem. I can't do anything about it, Reina."

But deep down Sarita was thankful that life was back to normal. Now she could go play bingo at six, flirt with Don Florencio, come home, talk to Panchito and watch her *telenovelas*. Panchito was her new canary. The pet shop salesperson had tried to sell her a cockatiel that pecked food from her palm. But Sarita bought a bright orange canary, a *macho* that sang beautifully. It had an uncombed top and would flutter around, extend its wings as if to tell her that it was too big for its cage. She named him after her favorite revolutionary.

Two weeks later, on a Sunday, Sarita could see a party going on in Matilde's patio. No one she recognized. She figured they were Gustavo's family, so she took out half a Jell-O mold from the fridge, sliced the mold into delicate pieces, arranged them on a platter, and went over. Gustavo had a chef's hat on and was burning the *carne asada*. He was all smiles. His grandmother was there. Her name was Socorro, but Gustavo called her Buelita Coro, which sounded stupid coming from Gustavo. But Sarita sat next to her anyway.

"My Gustavo is such a good boy," the woman started off.

"Really?" Sarita replied.

"He works so hard. He makes me so proud. And I know that Matilde will take good care of him."

"Hmm."

"You must see them all the time. I'm so envious. I only see them twice a month. You know, I live so far."

"I hear them more than see them."

"I live in Riverside, you know."

"I said I hear them more than see them."

"It's about an hour drive to Riverside, and in traffic, maybe two. He's such a good boy never to forget his grandmother. He's not like his father, that's for sure. I'm sorry, what did you say?"

"I said that I don't really get to see them that much either. I do hear them, though, when Gustavo beats her, usually after they make love, but sometimes before and then they make love—you know—but that other day when he hit her and Matilde lost the baby, that day I got to see both of them, but it's still not as much as you see them."

The woman gasped for air, looked around the room to see who had heard. Sarita rose from her lawn chair, placed her half-filled glass of iced tea on the table, and quietly walked out. She sighed and then softly said to herself, "That's for not singing at your funeral, even though I promised."

Sarita stood in her bedroom closet looking at dresses. She brought out three and laid them on the bed. Don Florencio was stopping by tonight to see the last episode of their favorite *telenovela,* "Pecado Mortal." Don Florencio had been stopping by for almost a year now, and Sarita always prepared a flan, but last time she burned it. It was quite embarrassing because Don Florencio, the gracious man that he was, insisted on eating the whole thing. "Today, Sarita," she whispered to herself, "you are going to use the timer when you make the flan. Who knows? He may be lucky number four."

Then she went to her living room window, pulled the drapes back, and saw Gustavo walking his pale grandmother to the car. His head was down, moving from side to side. He was denying everything.

"Like the coward that you are," Sarita muttered to herself.

When Gustavo extended his hand to help sit her in the back seat, his grandmother pulled away from him. Gustavo stood there with a look of despair. It was probably the first time his Buelita Coro had ever rejected him. He stood there motionless, looking down as the car drove off.

About ten minutes later, the doorbell rang. Sarita had barely turned the lock when Gustavo slammed his way through the door. His arm pushed hard against Sarita, who fell to the ground. Her elbow hit the side of the sofa. Gustavo stared at Sarita on the floor, then he left. Sarita could feel a pain in her back and in her arm, at first intense but then slowly subsiding. Matilde walked into the house and screamed when she saw Sarita.

"Call the police!" Sarita yelled.

"Please don't," Matilde sobbed.

"Will you leave him?" Sarita asked. This time her voice was soft. It was more of a request than a question.

Matilde stammered as she broke out in a wail, "He, he, he says he's going to marry me!"

Sarita looked at her, then up at the ceiling. She was trying to find the words to explain it to Reina but couldn't. Sarita closed her eyes and said quietly to Matilde, "Go home, little girl."

Sarita sat in the kitchen, rubbed her elbow with Ben Gay, and then poured some tequila into her coffee cup and drank it slowly. She could hear Panchito fluttering from one side of his cage to another. She watched the canary as it would occasionally body slam itself against the wire. Sarita took scissors from her sewing basket and went to the birdcage. Her hand chased the bird until she caught him.

"Panchito," she told him, "this is so you can be outside of your cage." She extended one wing and then clipped it. "You would rather live outside of the cage, no?" she said as she clipped the other. Sarita put Panchito back into the cage, went to the windowsill, and poured herself another tequila.

"Sing for me, Panchito," she yelled to the bird. But the bird lay still on the floor of its cage. "Tomorrow, you'll feel better. I know it takes getting used to."

She dialed the phone. Gustavo answered.

"Gustavo," Sarita said, "don't ever come near my house. I've called people and told them what happened. And they will go to the police if I can't. But that's not why I called you. Do you want to know why I called you, little boy?"

Gustavo's raspy voice reluctantly said, "Why?"

"Because I want you to know that Matilde has told me everything, even about how you make love to her, that you have to look at yourself in the mirror to get it up, that even then you can't. That's why you hit her. You're not a man. You're a *pinche cobarde*! Do you hear me? You're a *pinche cobarde* and that's not all she's told me . . . ."

Sarita heard the click. She put the receiver down and stood there for a minute before she picked it up again and called 911. Yes, a crime was going on next door. No, she couldn't give details, but the police should come over *inmediatamente*. It was a matter of life and death. Click again.

Sarita went over to the doors and made sure the deadbolts had been fastened. Then she went to the living room. She could hear Gustavo yelling at Matilde, "YOU TOLD HER?" She heard things breaking, the lamp maybe or maybe the vanity mirror. She could hear Matilde yelling, "Please, Gustavo, please!"

She walked to her turntable and blew the dust off the album. A familiar scratchiness sounded as the needle touched the vinyl. An old noise that took her back. She turned the volume knob all the way up. The yearning in Lola's voice was her own. A yearning so strong that Sarita had to close her eyes. And there in the darkness suddenly appeared her husbands. A slide show of images. Men smiling, men holding her, men making love to her. Then she saw Reina. She saw Reina's beautiful smile, a smile as penetrating as Lola's voice. The music permeated every pore and resonated with the pains and passions in her soul. Reina would forgive her. Sarita raised her palms to her chest. Slow. And sad. She broke into song.

Count the Raindrops

I. *Count the raindrops*—10 p.m. Saturday

I was on a Greyhound bus headed for Los Angeles from Seattle when my dream jolted me awake. My fingers pressed hard against my forehead as I realized that right there on my blue-cushioned seat and in front of God and everyone, I had orgasmed in my sleep.

I looked around and noticed that no one was sitting near me, and that was a good thing, if only because it is a tremendously awkward feeling to come in one's sleep—at least for me. See, I hadn't actually experienced the orgasm, not consciously anyway, but I knew I had had one because I felt the pulsations, the spasms happening between my legs. There had been no pleasure. There never was.

What was I dreaming? I tried hard to remember. My dreams are usually long, vivid narratives, but this one wasn't. This one was just an image. And I could only remember a part of it. I was squatting and rubbing two sticks together as if I was trying to make fire. It didn't make any sense to me.

I sat there completely confused by my body. And just as ashamed by the lack of control I had over it. As I waited for the spasms to subside, I pushed forward softly, almost in a rocking motion, as if to tell myself that it was okay.

I had only had one real orgasm in my entire life, and that had been several years ago in a dorm room with a college boy I had really cared for, maybe even loved. I couldn't even remember his last name anymore.

My bus had just crossed the Oregon border, and it was still raining hard. I didn't know why I was going home. I only knew I shouldn't stay away any longer. I couldn't, really. Something precious had been taken away from me years ago, and I wasn't sure what it was. Maybe my happiness, maybe peace of mind. Whatever it was, I was going home to reclaim it.

The next stop was thirty minutes in Portland. It was as good a time as any to get off and call my mother and let her know I was on my way. I didn't want to make the call. But I didn't know what else to do. The only one who had ever given me courage was my grandmother. When she was alive, she had a beautiful way of bottom-lining things and making them okay. With ferocity, she would shout out words like *I love you* or *We're family* or *Let's have faith in God,* and that would resolve things. It would resolve everything. She died when I was twelve. In some ways, I needed her so much more than my mother. Now, the only thing that calms me is three shots of gin, sometimes four.

It was, therefore, no coincidence that at this moment of ambivalence in front of the pay phone, I summoned my grandmother's image to guide my fingers and make the call.

"Mom, I'm coming home," I said.

"Where've you been?" she asked. "Your phone's been disconnected."

"Probably tomorrow afternoon, maybe tomorrow night."

"Come home then," she said. There was hurt in her voice.

"I had a run-in with the police."

"What for?"

"Drunkenness."

"Why were you drinking?"

"I don't know. What does it matter?"

"You need to come home now. You need to not stay away any longer. Do you hear me?"

"And Skid?"

"Your brother wants you home as much as I do."

"I'm not staying in the same house."

"Your brother loves you."

"I'm not staying."

"What do you want me to do? Throw him out, so I can let you in?"

"Does he have a real job?"

"Preaching the word of the Lord is the best job there is."

"You've always covered for him."

"Somebody has to. I'm his mother. If anyone, it should be me."

"I'll stop by, but I'm not staying. Tell him I don't want to see him when I get there tomorrow night."

My brother Skid had decided to follow in my father's footsteps and take up the ministry, and I was furious to the point of disowning him.

My mother and Skid lived in a poorly kept Victorian home off Rampart Boulevard in Los Angeles. I had grown up there but had left for college when I turned eighteen. I could have gone to college closer to home, but I wanted nothing more than to move away. And I did move out the day after I turned eighteen—the same year my father became ill. I hadn't seen him since, even though he lived just down the street from my mother.

My father used to be a really popular preacher at the Pentecostal Believers in Christ Temple. He had an active congregation of maybe a thousand people, most of them immigrants from Mexico and Central America. My father was handsome. People said he resembled Desi Arnaz, fair skinned and clean shaven. Always in a suit. Always singing. But everything changed when he got sick.

My father had performed a prayer service for a man, a Mexican immigrant, who had died of some contagious disease. Apparently, he had swum through a sewer in order to cross the border. Some said it was the water. Others said he had been attacked by rats in the sewer.

When my father went out and found the body in a shack behind a tenement building, the man had already been dead a few days. His family didn't want to take him to the hospital because they were afraid of the authorities. The room was very small, and the smell of the dead man made him feel claustrophobic.

Two weeks later, my father's face swelled up, and then it turned purple, an ugly dark purple. His skin tightened and became glossy like an eggplant.

But the worst part was that his tongue swelled up, too. So much that he couldn't close his mouth entirely. In fact, part of his tongue protruded from his lips. An alley punk from the neighborhood nicknamed my father "La Pupusa," because his face resembled the female sex organ.

My father stayed a week in the hospital until the doctors finally diagnosed him with a rare skin disease. The disease left him without speech, and as much as his congregation loved him, they had to deal with the reality of replacing him. My father tried overcoming his disease by purchasing an expensive amplifier and a new microphone for the pulpit. But it was no use. His speech was at best barely over a whisper, and eventually he was replaced. And who would end up replacing him? Of all the pastors, in all of the churches, in all the city, it had to be my brother.

When all of this was happening, my mother asked my father to move out of the house. He refused, but she threatened to speak to the congregation about him. So he moved to our back house, which had originally been a work shed that had been remodeled into a single studio unit. He stayed there for over a year, but I guess that was still too close, so Mom evicted him by telling him that if he didn't move out, she'd file for divorce.

That's when he moved into the storage room in the Temple. He converted it into his bedroom and insisted that the members of the congregation refer to it as his *rectoría*.

I had heard that he spent his days polishing the pews and the piano and arranging the flowers around the podium. When it was time for the service, the handsome young men in the congregation would stand by the doors and greet the church members while my father was in the back room pushing a button on the wall that sounded off electrical bells.

II. *Little girl, you're through*—2:00 a.m. Sunday

I had been working a double shift at the Barnes & Noble on Clover Street for over a year. I thought if I saved enough, I could rent a place near campus and drum up the courage to reapply. I'd have to drag my ass back to see Mr. Espinoza, my counselor and friend. Mr. Espinoza was a crotchety old man whose biggest kick was helping poor kids like me get through college. He had tried so hard to keep me in school, but I kept screwing up. Every time he had to help me petition for readmission, I'd let him let me have it. He'd tell me what a loser I was, what a shame I was to my family, to my people, and all the rest, and then he'd do everything possible to get me back in. It would be my third hiatus from school. I was twenty-seven, and I still hadn't finished my B.A. "If you're determined to stay here permanently," Mr. Espinoza told me, "I'll get you a job as a counselor, but get your goddamn B.A., okay? Get the goddamn degree. Just get the *pinche* degree!"

I liked working at Barnes & Noble because it was easy to get picked up by professional men. The dates usually included a free dinner and a lot of booze. They would get what they wanted, and so would I. Anyway, I got to read as many books as I wanted. A lot of them weren't in the library yet.

Every day, all day, I spent behind the information desk. You'd think that you'd get a lot of people asking questions, but I sat behind the desk for hours at a time with nothing but a cup of coffee and a book. Every once in a while, the job gave me too much time to myself, and I'd get to thinking about my life, and it was not a good thing. Really, that was the only job hazard.

Rudy, the guy in the music section, had a crush on me, and he'd try to get my attention all the time. He said he liked me 'cause I was a college girl. I had to keep on telling him that I dropped out, and he'd always reply that with my interest in books I was going back. "No question about it."

"If you're so interested in school," I told him, "then why don't you apply?"

He explained that he had a kid brother that he needed to look out for. His parents had come from Oaxaca to Washington to pick apples. They lasted in Spokane for ten years, then got fed up with the weather and decided it was time to go back home, but Rudy didn't want to, and his kid brother was an honors student.

So Rudy stayed, quit community college, and got a job. He worked so his brother could go to school. "He's only got another year and then he's off," he said. "He'll get a scholarship, and I'll have time for myself."

I admired how he took everything so lightheartedly, even though he hadn't had it easy. Rudy always found a way to smile about things, to reconcile them, to blow them off.

"Then you should apply," I'd tell him.

"Only if you go back," he'd say.

Two nights ago, Rudy and I had planned to take out Chinese food and go to my place. Rudy had "borrowed" some CDs from the shop, and we were going to try them out. I was behind my desk absorbed in the last chapter of a murder mystery when I heard a song. At first it sounded like a Christmas song, which is unusual since we don't start playing Christmas music until mid-November. It was a jazz tune, a soulful, sad one, and it reminded me of a lullaby. The woman's voice and the sound of the piano keys carried me somewhere. I could see the white piano keys, and I then realized I knew the notes by heart. Without thinking, I grabbed my coat and walked out. I was halfway down the block when Rudy came running after me. "Hey, you lunatic, were you planning to leave without me?"

"No, I just needed some fresh air. I was starting to feel all cramped up behind that desk."

So we went and ordered lo mein and mu shu pork and went to my apartment to hang out, only after we ate, Rudy decided to wash my dishes (I had quite a pile going) while I cleaned up my living room. I had shoes and towels thrown on the floor and sofa.

He insisted that he wanted to make room to dance. He had some samba CD's, and he said he wanted to check out my dance steps. He teased me that bookworms had a tendency to have two left feet. But I told him that even if he didn't see it, I had music deep down in me. No one could touch my rhythm, I told him.

"Come here," he said, and he grabbed me close and showed me his moves. And they were very hot. The man could move his hips with an ease and grace that made me think dirty thoughts. I thought of how I wanted those hips to flow that way beneath me. And when a love ballad played, he grabbed me even closer, and we slow-danced. His lips occasionally touched my neck. He wasn't kissing me. His face was just there—between my shoulder and the side of my face.

And then he made the terrible mistake of whispering into my ear, a plea that he was lonely, that he needed me, that he was falling for me. And then he called me his *reina*. "*Mi reina, mi amor*," he whispered into my ear.

I cringed and ran out of the apartment and into the chilly night without a jacket. And I just kept running. And when I heard him shouting out my name behind me, I told him to leave me alone. To get the hell away from me. I kept running until I found a bar and then another one, and then I found a man who bought me drinks at this dive called Escape the Ape.

I don't remember much after that. I don't remember how I paid for my drinks or how many I had. I do remember that there was a neon gorilla with a martini glass that went on and off, on and off. And that I kept nagging the bartender for another and another.

The cops picked me up for vagrancy, and they took me in and booked me. They told me they would keep me there until Sunday. It was Friday night. A tall, white, ugly, baton-up-his-ass cop asked me if there was someone I wanted to call. I looked for strength to refuse the phone call.

The cop smirked, "All alone, are you?"

Without really thinking I shouted out Rudy's number. It was early morning. "Hey, what's up?" he said calmly.

I told him I was in jail, that I just needed to talk to someone.

"Do you want me to call your parents?" he asked.

"No," I answered.

"I'll do what I can," he responded. A few hours later, they released me. Rudy was waiting outside. The dark circles beneath his eyes seemed as dark as mine. I was surprised that he was able to post bail for me.

"I had to show my tax return and cough up a thousand dollars," he said to me just outside the police station. "I make enough to file a tax return, if you can believe that."

"How did you come up with the money?" I asked him.

"My kid brother's scholarship money. It's just money," he said.

"I'm leaving Seattle," I told him. "It'll be a while before I can pay you back."

"I love you," he said to me.

"I'm not coming back," I said to him.

"I'll follow you," he said to me.

I kissed him once on the cheek and gave him a tight hug. But then I broke down, and he held onto me. He kissed my forehead and then my lips. And then I said good-bye and walked away. I walked for hours and hours until I went home. When I got to my apartment, I couldn't sleep. There wasn't anything in the cupboards, so I couldn't eat. And because the phone had been disconnected, I couldn't call anyone. The thought entered my mind that I needed to go home because I could no longer take care of myself. Of course, I was terrified. So I packed my old book bag with some T-shirts and jeans and headed for the bus station.

"Am I a good girl, daddy?" I asked him.

"You're the best girl, my favorite girl," he replied as he lay beside me.

"On the outside and the inside?" I replied crying.

"On the outside and the inside," he replied as his fingers touched me all over.

He was a wonderful piano player, singing praises to the Lord with a grace and a melody that left the congregation mesmerized. When the service was over and the temple was empty, he'd sit me next to him on the piano bench and tell me that because I was his *reina*, he was going to play some special songs for me, and he'd start with hymns, then some Spanish love songs, and then he'd sing me some lullabies. Eventually, I'd join him on the piano and then in the singing. My white patent leather shoes could barely touch the foot pedal. I already knew over fifty hymns by heart. At dinner, he'd constantly tell me how proud of me he was, of how I was his prodigy.

"Will I go to heaven?" I would always ask.

"Of course, my sweet," he always answered.

III. *Ain't no use, old girl*—Four hours later

When we were on our bikes on our way to the 7-Eleven, I told my brother Skid my special secret. He was three years older than me, and he had a ten-speed. I had to pedal furiously to keep up with him as he seemed to glide with ease in front of me.

When we got to the 7-Eleven, he bought me my slurpie in silence. At the park, we sat on opposite ends of a tree trunk slurping silently until he asked me, "Does it hurt?"

I told him everything, and he turned away from me and started to cry. I reached out my hand, and he held it tight. That afternoon, he cried as much as I did.

It happened seven times after that. After dinner, my father would order everyone including my mother to bed early. We would pray privately, he said, so that each family member could make a personal plea for intercession.

My father would go into the laundry room, and you could hear him arguing with God, shouting out names. Sometimes I'd hear his hand pounding on the washing machine. The hollow sound he made when his hand slammed on the metal made me cringe beneath my blankets.

It was as if good and evil were at odds in that room. But evil always won because he always came to me afterwards.

And every time it happened, I'd wait for someone to save me. Once, when he was in the room with me, I saw two spots in the strip of light coming in from beneath my bedroom door. They were Skid's feet. I knew they were.

I thought any minute now my big brother would run into the room and rescue me, but he never did. For all those times it happened, Skid just stood there beyond the door, waiting, perhaps as much as I was, for the night to finish. My world had been crystallized by that one inaction. My peace of mind was that light just beyond the door; it was that knock that never happened.

I sat restlessly in my seat as I thought about the baseball bat my mother kept by the fireplace. The bat had been used, as far as I could remember, only twice by my grandmother to chase the bums who slept on a grassy area in our backyard. She let them sleep there and even occasionally fed them, but when they started leaving their drug paraphernalia for us to see, she booted them off the property.

I thought that the first thing I would do when I arrived in Los Angeles would be to walk into the house, reach for the bat, and then walk those long three blocks to the temple. I would walk by the altar, through the back door, across the patio, and find my father. And then with all my might, I would swing the bat at him. Swing it at that fucking eggplant monster.

When I was a little girl, he'd buy me a piñata for my birthday. He did that until I was fourteen. The older I got, the fewer hits it took to rip it open. I'd examine the swinging papier-mâchéd pig above me, measuring its movements, anticipating the exact angle, the weakest spot, so that one crucial hit would burst the thing open.

That's what I wanted to do to his head. Burst it open. Smash it open. Swing into it relentlessly, so that the game would finally be over.

The bus made a ten-minute stop in Stockton. A large woman with a beaming smile sat across from me. She was wearing a cream-colored dress suit, with a matching hairnet around her bun. I fidgeted in my seat because my stomach was still very queasy. I had thrown up several times in the last two days, and my stomach and throat hurt from the heaving. I knew I looked very pale.

"Are you all right?" she said to me.

"Stomach flu," I said.

"Those flus can be nasty," she responded.

She reached below the seat in front of her, took out a 7-Up from her bag, and then from her purse a Tylenol medicine bottle. "Take two of these and drink this. Sometimes, all you really need is rest."

I thanked her and took her advice, but closing my eyes just brought back bad memories. I tried to replace them with blankness, but my brain insisted on taking me back there. When my eyes refused to take in painful memories, my ears became more acute, and my fingers moved to the keys of the lullaby. With my right hand, I tried to remember the first couple of bars.

When I felt my breathing getting harder, I opened my eyes and looked at the woman. "Going back home?" I asked her.

"Leaving home actually. Home is Stockton. I'm going to a wedding. My husband's first child is getting married tonight in Compton. He's already down there with my little girl. They flew down last week, but I couldn't get that much time off from work. I'm a counselor. I do crisis intervention at a battered women's center. Anyway, I had to wait until today. I'm just so excited and so tired."

The whole time we were talking a young guy talked into his phone. He wasn't speaking English. I thought he might be Indian. I had an Indian roommate when I lived in the dorms during my first year of college, and it sounded the same way.

He'd speak normal and then lower his voice and pull the cell closer to him. I glanced a couple of times to look at him when he'd start whispering into the phone. I could tell that he noticed me noticing him, so he turned and faced the window while he continued talking. When we got to San Francisco, he pulled out a laptop case from above his seat and three duffel bags full of stuff and rushed clumsily off the bus.

The bus was in the San Francisco bus station for at most ten minutes. As we were pulling out of the parking lot, I saw the same young guy running toward the bus, waving his hands at us, but the bus driver must have not seen him because he just kept driving.

I turned back to where he had been sitting and saw his cell phone on the seat. I interrupted the woman next to me as she chattered away and grabbed the phone on my way to the toilet.

IV. *Why won't somebody send a tender, little blue boy?*
—12:00 p.m. Sunday

The bus toilet was filthy. It reeked of urine. It was an intense, penetrating smell. I pulled out the cell phone. The battery was still working.

I dialed home. "There was an hour delay in Stockton," I said as soon as I recognized my mother's voice. My mother was steady, but she wasn't strong like my grandmother. Her love for my father, for her role as a pastor's wife, had made her so passive, too concerned about what the others in the congregation thought.

"That's okay. Just call us when you're closer to Los Angeles so we can pick you up," my mother replied.

"I'll take a taxi," I said.

"What for?" my mother said. "They're so expensive, anyway. I told Skid you're coming home. He took me to buy some meat and *masa* for tamales. I'm making your favorite kind. He's right here. Talk to him." It had been years since I had spoken to my brother.

My heart sank, and I put the phone down, and then held it up to my ear again. I heard my brother say, "Hey kiddo, how are you holding up?"

"Hey," was all I said.

"Mom said you didn't want to see me. You must not miss me the way I miss you. I love you, you heartbreaker."

My brother had my father's gift for speech. He could say things like that without his voice changing a bit, as though it were something chatty, some by-the-way thing. I, on the other hand, felt like someone had just performed a tracheotomy on me. My head pushed against the metal plate that served as the sink mirror as I broke down.

"You were behind the door the whole time, weren't you?" I cried.

"What do you mean?"

"You stayed behind the door. You stayed even after I told you! How could you leave me with him?"

"I didn't know what else to do. What could I do?"

My voice got high as I sucked in snot. "You asshole, how could you be like him? How could you grow up to be just like him?"

"The Lord helps me find the strength to not be like him. It sure pains me how much I disappoint you."

"Is Mom standing next to you?" I asked.

"She's right here," he responded.

"What's she look like?"

"What do you mean?"

"What does she look like?"

"Her hair's up like always. She's got her long denim skirt on. She's wearing her tamale apron."

"Take a good look at her. I will NEVER be like that. Do you understand? I'll never be like that. I'll never be like her."

"Sweet pea, I'll make it up to you. It's been hard without you. Really hard. Sure looking forward to seeing you."

I wondered if I had misread the evenness in my brother's tone. There was something very wrong in the tone of his voice. Some lack of feeling, lack of presence. It resembled the evenness he had been using seven years ago when he had accidentally cut his neck shaving.

It was stupid to pretend that Skid had cut himself by accident that one time. He was seventeen and was getting all sorts of pressure by my father to go to ministry school. My father had to break down the bathroom door when they saw blood coming out from under it. Skid was on the floor, unconscious. When they asked him why he hadn't shouted for help or something, Skid said that when it happened, he was in such a state of shock that he didn't know how to react, and then he must have lost consciousness. My mother had insisted that it was an accident and went out of her way to explain her version of the occurrence to every member of the congregation, especially to the choir women whom she thought might gossip otherwise. If Skid was with her, he'd agree with my mother and joke that he was just trying to be as clean-shaven as my father.

It occurred to me that perhaps the real reason I was going home was because my brother needed me. I used to call him my pet turtle because he always pulled into himself. No one ever really knew what was going on in Skid's head, except me. He always told me the truth. Everyone accepted Skid's distance as a quiet eccentricity. It was good enough that he was kind hearted, patient, and dutiful.

Something protective, maternal, and fierce swelled up in me at the thought of my brother being in trouble. There was a bond between us, a bond that was stronger than me, one neither of us could deny. How could I have forgotten someone so important to me? I realized at that moment I'd do anything for my brother. Even maybe forgive him.

I turned around to face the toilet when I thought I was going to vomit again. I heaved, but only a thick glob of saliva came to my mouth. There was nothing in my stomach to vomit. I felt like I might faint.

When I went to sit down, the woman stared at me and said, "You're going to need to go to a doctor as soon as you get home. You just don't look good."

"I'll be all right," I said. "Why'd you become a counselor?"

"'Cause I knew I'd be good at it. I have something to tell others, I guess," she responded.

"I was a psychology major in school," I said. "I was pretty good at it."

"You didn't finish?" she asked.

"No, I kept getting kicked out of school. I was always drinking and partying. Forgetting to attend classes . . . and I'd fail nearly all of them. When I was sober, I'd get good grades, though. Then I lost my scholarship money and that was it."

"Never thought of changing your life?" she asked.

"Not yet," I responded.

"Guess you ain't suffered enough," she said, matter of fact.

"Guess not," I said. I thought to myself, What does this bitch know about suffering? Fucking self-righteousness came out of a crack like a cockroach.

"You need to find faith in the Lord," she said to me.

Now I really hated her. I thought for a second about what to say to her, but she was the least of my worries, and so I said nothing.

Then the cell phone in my pocket began to vibrate. I sat up, heaved painfully, and then excused myself and headed for the toilet again. There I clicked on the cell phone. It was a woman who was speaking Hindi to me. When I answered in English, she raised her voice in a broken English. What was I doing with her husband's cell phone? Who the hell was I? Where was her husband?

"Excuse me, wrong number," I said and hung up on her. Then I dialed the bookstore in Seattle. When Rudy heard my voice, he said, "Where are you, you lunatic?"

"I'm on a bus to Los Angeles."

"Were you kidding about not coming back?"

"No, I wasn't," I responded.

"I wasn't either."

"You weren't either what?"

"I wasn't kidding when I said I'd follow you."

"Why do you love me?"

"I don't know. Because you need me. Because you're pretty. Because you're smart. Do you need to know more?"

"I guess not."

"You have a court date."

"I know," I responded.

"Let me come get you, and then when that's over, I'll take you back to Los Angeles. Then you can stay there."

"I don't love you," I said. "At least not yet."

"Then forget it. Just forget it. Forget the whole damn thing."

My stomach knotted at the thought of losing him.

Then he said, "Just *kidding*."

I laughed. My body resisted it, but the knot loosened. I felt affection for him, tenderness, some sugar-rush kind of feeling.

I clicked the phone off, but as soon as I got back to my seat, it started vibrating again. Who could it be? A crazed wife shouting a language I didn't know, my brother, or maybe it was Rudy. I'd leave it in my pocket for now.

The bus driver had a boom box playing country music. He didn't have the music loud, but I could still hear it. Behind the twangy voice and guitars, there was an audible drumbeat. I focused in on the drumbeat. It would carry me somewhere. To a good memory for a change. This time, I'd make my mind listen to me. I'd focus on the wheels of the bus, focus on how they were rolling on the asphalt. They were moving, going south, and I was going home.

The Cross

"María Elena, for Christ's sake, you're a middle-aged woman," he said smugly.

And with that, she punched him. Hard. Once above the bridge of his nose. Her wedding ring, a diamond, cut right through his skin. Pierced it. And when she punched him again, she ripped open his forehead as if she had a scalpel. Blood spewed out everywhere.

The waiter ran to offer the man a dish towel. "Professor, are you all right?" he said. "Are you all right? Call an ambulance!"

Meanwhile, the professor's wife, María Elena, leaned against the bar stool clutching her heart.

The paramedics took them both in the ambulance. Side by side. María Elena died of heart failure that same night. Her husband was patched up. "Ten stitches," the doctor said. It left a dent on his forehead. From up close it looked like a cross.

My mother and my Aunt Matilde were devastated. They claimed that their sister didn't have congestive heart failure, but that her motherfucking philanderer of a husband killed her.

My mother's family is from the Texas border, on the Mexican side. And they were not satisfied that my uncle came out of that situation with only a few stitches. The way my family saw it, it was an eye for an eye. At the funeral, my mother cried out that we should tie my Uncle Alfonso to his black convertible and drag his ass by the Los Angeles River till the fucker was dead. It was a good thing he left the funeral service early because my mother's sedative was wearing off, and she and my Aunt Matilde were talking about getting my cousins to jump him.

It was my Aunt Matilde who came up with the idea of *brujería*. She said, "He's already a hypochondriac. We'll torture him just by letting him know that we're doing witchcraft on him. We'll tell him that we're putting his picture upside down in a glass of water and praying to the devil that his cock falls off."

My mother, my Aunt Matilde, and my Aunt María Elena were really tight. The three of them were always together, like the holy trinity. They were not just sisters; they were best friends. Each was the others' confidante and spiritual advisor. When one had heartache, they all had heartache. When one had a child, it belonged to all of them. (I belonged to all of them.)

But now a third was missing, and there was nothing they could do. It didn't matter how strong they were, or how smart they were, or how hard they worked. They couldn't bring María Elena back. It was the helplessness that drove them mad, so they clung to this strange idea of bewitching my Uncle Alfonso.

Anyway, I was the only one that was there when it happened. I was the one in the ambulance, the one who held María Elena by the shoulders, who kissed her temple, who rocked her helplessly in my arms. It's been over a year now that she's been dead, and it still seems like yesterday.

I wasn't doing well in school and my Aunt María Elena, a college English instructor, decided to tutor me because I had been kicked out of honors English. I was really upset about it because I had the ambition of becoming a writer some day. She was the only one I had quietly confessed this to.

When she found out about my being dropped from class, she went out of her way to arrange a weekly tutoring schedule. Every Wednesday, we'd go to the public library where she'd give me time to work on my drafts and then look over my essays. After the tutorial, we'd go out to dinner.

We were at a Marie Calender's having dinner and talking about college when my aunt looked out the window and saw my uncle pull up in his new black Mustang convertible. (They had had a terrible argument over the new convertible since my uncle had a perfectly well functioning Honda.) Both my aunt and I saw the valet attendant dramatically open the door for the young woman who was in the car with my uncle. She had a shiny teal tube top with black shorts and high-heel slip-ons. Her hair was everywhere, and she wore too much eyeliner and lipstick. I thought she was a hooker, but later we found out that she was a student of his. I caught my breath as I saw the two walk arm in arm into the fancy sports bar/athletic club across the street.

My aunt stared out the window looking at her husband with this bimbo, but she didn't say anything to me. She sat composed and asked the waitress for the check. Then, she pushed her pie away and said, "*M'ija*, life is so boring, you know, so few things in it are truly satisfying." She paused. "That's why you have to live alone and find your passion. Don't get married young. There are too many assholes out there, and you're too young to tell who's who. Otherwise, you'll end up like me."

When the check came, she placed a twenty-dollar bill on the table, asked me to wait for her there, and got out of the booth without saying one more word to me.

I didn't dare follow her. But then I saw the bimbo run out of the bar. She stumbled at the street corner and had to lean against the stoplight in order to adjust her high heels, but then she kept on running.

I couldn't contain my worry and so I ran across the street and into the sports bar. There, I saw my aunt slumped back on the bar, her hand over her heart. My uncle had blood dripping all over his face. His one hand touched his forehead while the other shook violently toward my Aunt María Elena. He touched his blood-stained shirt, his fancy blazer, and said over and over, "I can't fucking believe you, María Elena!" Only my aunt wasn't listening to him anymore. She had lost consciousness. She may have already been dead.

I want to stress the point that my mother and my aunt didn't really practice witchcraft. They just wanted my Uncle Alfonso to think they did. What did they know about *brujería,* anyway? They were born in the United States. But they remembered when my grandmother and great-grandmother would talk about *brujas* turning people into turkeys and making beautiful women's legs rot and about people going blind on account of someone giving them the evil eye. My grandmother used to say that it was a good idea to be nice to people, and she wasn't talking about being a good Christian or anything like that; she was talking about if you were an asshole and you pissed off the wrong person, you could ruin the rest of your life or your family's.

Like my great-aunt Carmen, who was fine one minute and the next got some unexplained palsy that contorted her face. Everybody said the town witch, Piedad, was sleeping with my great-aunt's husband. The townspeople claimed that Piedad prayed to the devil to mess up my great-aunt's face so her husband wouldn't touch her anymore. And it worked because her husband left her and my great-aunt never married again.

Anyway, these were the tales my mother and, to some extent, I grew up with. And my mom knew that Uncle Alfonso had grown up on them too. And if someone said to him that he was *embrujado*, he'd get nervous. So that's what they did. They sent him little reminder notes of the things they were doing to him: an article on *brujería*, a lock of hair, a shoebox filled with some really foul smelling herb. In a frenzied fit of anger, my mother sent my Uncle Alfonso a picture of himself, only she did a cut-and-paste job, so my uncle's head had a monkey's body with long arms and legs and some other animal's curved dick. It was bizarre.

Of course, when you do shit like this it's bound to get out of hand. It didn't take my uncle that long to figure out who was sending him all this stuff, so he went to the police. But that didn't stop Mom or my Aunt Matilde. They just got more sophisticated. They e-mailed him messages from the public library or Kinko's and gave his home and e-mail address to fortune-tellers, tarot clubs, and *santería* shops. Mom put him on at least a hundred mailing lists of every voodoo catalog she could find. She was obsessed with this, and eventually it started to affect her relationship with Dad. He was really pissed off at her, but he put up with it for a while because he was still really in love.

But Mom hated Dad, I guess because he was a man, and that was enough. She'd get in his face and accuse him of lying to her, of cheating, of being "like all the rest." I felt sorry for Dad. I really did. Mom just didn't want him anymore. All she could talk about was my poor Aunt María

Elena and the payback that lowlife, philandering, motherfucker husband of hers was going to get.

A year after my aunt died, Dad left for Tucson and my parents filed for divorce. Mom decided to take a teaching job in San Francisco. She rented a place in the woods in Marin County above Stinson Beach and planned to commute to San Francisco. The thought of my mother in the woods concocting deranged plans to revenge her sister's death felt really wrong to me, so when she asked me to go with her, I said no. I just couldn't handle her anymore.

So she took my Aunt Matilde with her instead. My Aunt Matilde had a very successful tire business, but that didn't stop her from leaving it or her husband. All she told my Uncle Greg was, "My sister needs me right now. And I don't know how long I'm going to be gone." Uncle Greg warned her that he wasn't going to live off lunch truck food forever, but she said she'd take her chances.

A week after my nineteenth birthday, on a warm April morning, I sat on the porch and saw my mother and my aunt drive off in their respective SUV's to northern California.

I didn't want to be in that big house alone, but what could I do? That big house was where I was raised, and it was the only thing that wasn't moving in my life. So I stayed and registered at the local junior college, the same junior college where my Uncle Alfonso had been teaching history for years.

Uncle Alfonso was very popular. He was handsome and suave, very suave, and when he opened his mouth he'd take you with him on dramatic journeys into American history. At times, during his lectures he'd pause and ask, "Where's the social justice?" and repeat mantras like this as if he was a preacher. At the end of his lectures he'd touch students' shoulders (the females more than the males) and point to a poster that had two huge words in bold black letters: "QUESTION AUTHORITY!" I didn't have a single female friend who had taken his class and wasn't totally in love with him.

I saw Uncle Alfonso occasionally on campus. He'd always smile, call me *m'ija* and ask me how I was doing. We never spoke about my Aunt María Elena or his womanizing or the night we spent at the hospital when my Aunt María Elena died. Something really devious and self-destructive in me made me call my mother and tell her every time I'd run into him, and every time it pissed her off righteously. What was I doing talking to that man? Didn't I know he was a murderer? How could I betray my Aunt María Elena that way? I tried to explain to her that I really didn't hate him, that he had never treated me bad. But she never listened. She insisted that this was a family thing, a femme thing. The moment I placed the phone receiver down, guilt would seize my heart.

Then I saw the bimbo that my Uncle Alfonso was with the night of my aunt's death. I was on campus doing homework when she sat down next to me and fidgeted with her skirt, trying, I guess, to get it to cover her knee.

She said to me, "You're Izzie, right?"

My real name is Hortencia Isadora Ortiz, after my great-grandmother, but the schoolteachers and the kids in my suburban neighborhood kept chopping it down until they got to a manageable "Izzie." Turned out that she was in the same lab class as me.

She told me that she hadn't realized how chickenshit my Uncle Alfonso had been to my aunt. That is, it hadn't occurred to her how chickenshit he was until he did it to her.

Funny how it isn't until something bad happens to you that you can get a broader perspective on things.

Apparently, after four months together and without warning, Uncle Alfonso told her he had "lost interest." When she begged for an explanation, he grabbed her purse, took out his apartment key, and shoved her out his door.

"I hate him," she said.

Her name was Toni, short for Antonieta. She was Portuguese and had a massive amount of frizzy hair. The evening I first saw her from across the street she looked exotic, but up close she looked like a girl, her cheeks a little pudgy, her lips thin and plain. But her eyes conveyed sweetness. As it turned out, we both always got to class a little early, so I got to know her a little better. I guess you could say we became friends. Though the truth is we only had one thing to talk about.

At home, I converted the mantle into an altar for my Aunt María Elena. On the mantle, I placed all my favorite pictures of her, and, on the floor just below it, I laid her favorite gold scarf (she loved scarves), two poems (Neruda's *A Desperate Song* and Van Morrison's *In the Beginning*), some CDs (Springsteen and Bob Dylan), and a candle of Saint Christopher, the patron saint of travelers.

Saint Christopher carried Christ across the dangerous river, and I came to realize that I loved my Aunt María Elena so much because she had helped carry me through adolescence, she had been my mentor and confidante.

Every week I'd buy fresh yellow flowers for my aunt. Yellow flowers because that was her favorite color. Sometimes I'd get daisies, sometimes sunflowers, if I was lucky, daffodils or tulips. When I wasn't lucky, I'd have no choice but to buy cheap yellow carnations.

Every morning I'd take a moment to think of her, to talk to her about the family, to ask her to help me bring things back together.

I don't know if my aunt was working through me or not, and I'm a little embarrassed to confess what happened next, but there was so much going on in my life, with Dad gone, and Mom gone, and their divorce, and my aunt dead, that I didn't really know where to turn. So I went to a *curandera* shop. I feel bad because the place I should have gone to was a church, but it's not like a priest has ever been able to console me. I was lonely. I needed my family. I wanted things to be the way they used to be.

I told Toni that I was serious about doing something to bring my family back together. She suggested group therapy, but I told her that I wanted advice from a *curandera*, and I asked her if she would go with me. It started off as a dare, really. But then we started driving around the East Side until we found one on Whittier Boulevard.

The shop had wall-to-wall posters of saints and *La Virgen,* and the counters were filled with amulets, herbs, prayer books, and candles. It seemed like the prayer shops I'd seen in the mission churches. A middle-aged woman walked in from the garden behind the shop and took us into a smaller room behind the counter. She was a plump woman with a softness to her features. I told her the whole story of my aunt's death and my mother's obsession. I told her I wanted to cure my mother of this obsession, that it had caused my father to leave, that there was a *muy mal espíritu* in our family.

The woman asked me, "Where do you think the *mal espíritu* lives?"

"In my uncle, señora," I responded.

"Well then, the evil spirit must be taken out of him," she responded. "He needs a *limpia*."

"How?" I asked.

"You have to clean him. Purge the evil spirits out of him," she said.

She pulled out what looked like a hand broom, like the kind you buy to sweep the car floor, only much coarser. She went to a cabinet full of papers and took out a prayer pamphlet and a little bottle.

"Say this one over and over while you rub him with ointment and ask the spirit to leave. Then try to brush it out of him. Sweep his chest, his stomach, his legs and arms. Shout out the prayer. Remember that you will be fighting against evil forces and you will need to stay strong."

I took the broom from the woman. "What if my uncle doesn't want to be cleaned?"

"It usually only works if he's willing, but you can try it. I'll give you a discount. Perhaps you can do it while he's asleep. You don't have to touch his body. Remember, you must believe in what you're doing. You have to read and believe everything in the prayer book. Only that will give you power."

Well, for two months after that, Toni and I would meet after lab class about how we could perform a *limpia* on my Uncle Alfonso. Kidnapping him was out of the question, though I knew my mother would bail me out in a nanosecond. The idea intrigued me, but the truth is I didn't have the backbone to do it. On the other hand, going to him and trying to convince him of his misguided ways also seemed ridiculous.

Then, Toni volunteered to sleep with him one more time, so she could perform the *limpia* while he slept. Of all of the suggestions, Toni's volunteering seemed if not the most reasonable at least the most tangible.

But as fate would have it, we didn't get to "clean" my uncle. Why? Because what goes around comes around. For all the screwing over that my Uncle Alfonso had done in all his life, he finally screwed himself. In a big way.

Exactly two and a half months after we went to the *curandera*, Uncle Alfonso was admitted to intensive care for a heart attack, just like my Aunt María Elena. But his wasn't congenital. He had provoked a heart attack from taking double doses of Viagra to keep up with all the college girls he was bringing home. The Viagra and the steroids he was taking for his biceps didn't mix well, and he started having palpitations. Of course, he ignored the warning signs.

One night, after an especially long lovemaking session, he started feeling ill. He got up and went to the kitchen for a glass of water. When he leaned against the sink, he realized that his heart wouldn't stop pounding and that although he was sweating profusely, he was terribly cold. That's when he collapsed and had a full-blown heart attack at the ripe age of fifty-two.

He claimed he had a vision. In front of him, he saw death's door opening. At that moment, he said he felt more dead than alive. His arms and tongue had frozen, and he was unable to yell or move toward the bathroom so as to wake the woman who was in his bed. At that moment, he asked God for forgiveness and lost consciousness.

He didn't wake up until he was in intensive care. I found out about all of this because while in intensive care he asked the nurse to call my mother. He told my mother about his vision and that he wanted her forgiveness, that he didn't want to leave this earth without being able to tie up his loose ends with the family.

When faced with his desperate plea for forgiveness, my mother stated that she felt she had no choice but to forgive him. When he straight-out asked, "Claudia, do you forgive me?" my mother said she felt that her heart yanked from her body. But when she muttered "Yes," she felt it was placed back into her chest.

My mother said that when she said yes, she thought of young Alfonso. She thought of the naïve, kind teenager who hung out with the three sisters, the boy who was completely in love with María Elena, the one who, when he was twenty-one, promised to take care of her for the rest of his life—not the liar, not the cheater, not the fearful man that he grew to be.

When I heard about my uncle's heart attack, I gave Toni the oils and the prayer pamphlet as souvenirs of our aborted attempt to fix him, but I kept the broom. After musing about where to put it, I finally decided to leave it next to the vanity mirror in my bedroom.

I've kept the altar and continue placing fresh flowers for my aunt. I have Saint Christopher well lit and have asked my Aunt María Elena to carry me through my first move from my parents' home. Although I am scared because I'm not sure where I am going, I know my aunt will take care of me. Eventually, I know I will return home.

Mom resigned from her teaching assignment up north and is coming home in six months, and while she and Dad aren't together, at least they're talking, and she seems willing to listen to what he has to say.

As for my Uncle Alfonso, he's doing pretty well too. I saw him the other day in the hallway leading to the cafeteria. He was coming out, and I was going in. We only had a chance to exchange smiles. He looked a lot older. His tight jeans revealed a small potbelly, and his biceps seemed loose, but his smile still conveyed the dynamic person he was. The scar on his forehead had darkened and grown more prominent, perhaps because of his receding hairline. It seemed permanently embedded in his skin.

My mother had told me he had bypass surgery and recovered pretty quickly, though with the help of a pacemaker. Everyone says it's affected his popularity with the girls. Who knows? But I don't hear the same rumors about his womanizing. In fact, the rumor I hear is that he's taking a sabbatical. They say he wants to throw himself into researching the cultural implications of *brujería* on contemporary communities in the Southwest. If you ask me, he's got plenty of research under his belt already.

My Little Tyrant Heart
Corazoncito tirano

"The joke goes like this," he said. "The townspeople are worried to death because it hasn't rained in thirteen months, and the crops are dying. In desperation, they go to the priest, and they say to him, 'Please, father, lend us your statue of the baby Jesus.' The priest asks, 'Why on earth do you want baby Jesus?' The townspeople reply, 'To ask him to bring us rain, to beg him for mercy.' So the priest lends the townspeople baby Jesus, and they parade him all around town. They pray to El Santo Niño Jesús, sing to him, burn candles and incense for him, and then they hold a vigil. A day after the vigil, it starts raining cats and dogs. Pouring rainstorms destroy the crops. I mean, they completely ruin everything. The townspeople gather and go again to the priest. But this time they don't want baby Jesus. They ask for Saint Joseph. The priest says to them, 'I already lent you baby Jesus, and he sent you what you wanted.' The townspeople answer, 'Yes, father, but now we want Saint Joseph.' The priest says, 'And why Saint Joseph?' The townspeople reply, 'So he can see the fucking mess his kid made.'

"The fucking mess. You get it? Saint Joseph!" Esteban threw his head back and slapped his hand on his leg, totally enjoying his own joke. This I'm telling you in English, but

Esteban told it to me in Spanish, and it's a lot funnier in Spanish. The punch line is *Para que vea las chingaderas que hizo su hijo.* Esteban repeated over and over *chingaderas.* "That Jesus," Esteban said, "he's a big joker." Esteban was a robust man with dramatic sideburns and a potbelly, and he took up most of the front seat.

When I looked in the rearview mirror, I saw that my father had slept through the entire joke. He had asked me to drive because I guess he didn't completely trust Esteban. He figured this was the best way to keep an eye on him on this ride to Delano, which is where we were going to deposit Esteban so he could make a new go of it because the town where Esteban was born and raised threw him out. Esteban had taken a three-day bus ride to Tijuana where he found a *coyote* to take him across the border for twelve hundred bucks, only Esteban didn't have any money, so yesterday he arrived at our suburban home in Arcadia, California, WITH the *coyote*, who demanded the money in cash.

That's when my father called me to go to our ATMs (four hundred each from his personal and business accounts and four hundred from mine), so he could pay the *coyote,* who, by the time I got there, was quite angry. I was expecting some evil-looking Mexican man, but the *coyote* turned out to be a blonde woman in a 700 Series BMW. She had made Esteban put on a Hawaiian shirt, baby-blue corduroy shorts, and worn Vans tennis shoes, so he could pass as her hubby. When I handed over the cash, she insisted that she wanted Esteban to turn over the South Bay "costume," so right in the dining room, Esteban had to strip down to his boxer shorts while my father looked in his closet for one of his olive-colored gardener uniforms, only Esteban's potbelly was huge, and he had to wear his shirt open. The ribbed lines of the muscle shirt stretched way over his belt buckle. I gave Esteban a brown grocery bag with three of my dead husband's denim shirts, the few clothing items I hadn't given to Goodwill.

"My husband's," I said as I gave him the bag.

He looked inside it and slowly pulled out the shirts and measured the sleeve of one against his arm. "Tell him thanks," he smiled.

I didn't have it in me. I almost always don't. So I went into the kitchen and started washing my father's dirty ice-cream bowls and coffee cups.

Anyway, Esteban was my father's good friend, probably his best friend. I sensed he was trying hard to do the right thing, but it was a difficult situation. Yesterday afternoon my father had told him he couldn't stay with us. He insisted that there was no work for him in Arcadia, and anyway, he wasn't familiar with the city way of life. "Remember you're not a city man. There are too many vices, too many temptations here. You're better off up north, working the land. That's what you know how to do, isn't it?"

My father could have refused to pay the money, and he could have closed the door in Esteban's face, but I think my dad felt he owed Esteban somehow. Maybe because of the rough life that Esteban had. Maybe because my dad's life has ended up more or less okay.

I knew about Esteban way before I ever met him because my father had told me his story several times when I was younger. My father is a man of few words. I never got a bedtime story out of him. But he did tell me the story of Esteban, which was hardly a ghost story since Esteban was a real man—though it effectively scared the shit out of me. Too bad I don't believe in ghosts anymore. Now I'm forty-two, a widow, and childless, and I wish some dead loved ones would visit me every once in a while and help me figure out my life, but they never do.

Esteban and my father grew up in a ranch in Central Mexico in the 1940s, and they were shit poor like most of the world at that time, so the women had to leave the ranch and look for work in the city as housekeepers. Esteban fell madly in love and married Inés, who was one of the women who left town to find work in the city. But Inés was only fifteen years old, and she wasn't really keen on being a *rancherita* with ten children. So she began an affair with the owner of the house where she worked. The townspeople knew what was going on because they would see Inés in the *mercado* or plaza with her lover, and they told Esteban about it, but he refused to believe them. A year passed, and my father insists that Inés became more and more beautiful. She wore city-girl dresses and walked a mile into town in nylons and heels, ignoring the dust clouds.

Well, Esteban did end up murdering Inés, but the townspeople complained that because they didn't see it coming it was pretty unsatisfying. They had been denied all the juicy details that had led up to the murderous act.

Apparently, on Good Friday, Inés came home for the weekend and cooked Esteban beans and shrimp patties. Esteban ate two full plates and told her how much he loved her and how happy he was to see her home. Then he reached for his machete and whacked her hard one time with it, and that nearly cut her head off. He dragged her down to the canal, right near the overpass, and left her there for Abusto, the town drunk, to find—finding the nearly beheaded beautiful woman dressed in a red polka-dot dress and torn nylons forced Abusto to become an evangelist and leave drink forever, but that's another story.

As soon as the military found the body, they went straight to Esteban. (Since the town was away from the city, the military, not the police, investigated murders.) They found Esteban eating the shrimp patty leftovers. He denied everything. Told them that he was waiting for Inés to walk through the door at any minute. But the *sargento* checked his machete carefully anyway, and asked Esteban when he had last used it.

Esteban responded, "*sargento,* you know very well that everyone has to have one. How else can we harvest the fields?"

But the *sargento* must have suspected something because he broke off the machete's black handle, and as they both watched closely, Inés's blood trickled slowly out. The *sargento* and Esteban eyed each other in a tense moment, and then Esteban confessed everything. He was sentenced to fifteen years, but only because Ines's lover was a *político*.

But the story didn't end there. Although Esteban admitted killing Inés, he refused to admit that she was dead. And then her head disappeared from the judge's barn. They never found the head, and to date, Esteban insists on speaking about her in the present tense. The townspeople, being the superstitious bunch that they are, reported sightings of Inés by the irrigation ditches.

So when Esteban returned to town after serving his time in prison, the townspeople wanted to kick him out. He lived in a hut by the canal and would walk up and down the canals and irrigation ditches, crying out for Inés. They all thought he had lost his mind.

The townspeople accused him of growing marijuana in his crops and then selling it to the *pandilleros*, but Esteban claimed that that wasn't true, that he worked hard, and that the land was rightfully his. Eventually, the townspeople took his land from him and sold it to themselves for dirt cheap. And they sent Esteban to an insane asylum, but only for five years because as soon as the money from his land ran out, the asylum sent him back.

"Panchito, I wish I could help your girl with the driving," Esteban told my father. My father's name is Francisco, Don Francisco to his workers, Francisco to my mother, Pancho to his compadres, and only Panchito to Esteban. I had never heard my father referred to in the diminutive, and it was irritating to my ear, but apparently not to my father because he reached his hand from the back seat and placed it on Esteban's shoulder.

"Don't worry about it," he told Esteban as I pulled over at the Burger King at Gorman to get a cup of coffee. Esteban hummed a song called "Dark and Serene Night." The only reason I know the song is because my father plays it endlessly on his CD player at home. "That's one of my father's favorites, too," I said to him.

"Oh, it's a beautiful song," he replied. "The darker the night, the calmer my soul. It's when the moon is out, that's when the light drives me crazy. I hope you don't have a crazy moon out here."

"I'm from the city," I replied. "We don't notice the moon."

"It's a good thing," he said, "because the moon follows me. You know, sometimes I think it's Inés. She always follows me."

"Don't look up."

"Oh no, then I wouldn't be able to see the moon," he replied.

"Then it won't drive you crazy."

"But I live for the moon," he said. "It's when I talk to Inés."

"Can't live with it, can't live without it," I said.

"It's true love," he said. "*Amor del bueno*."

I drove into the Burger King and looked for parking. In the side-view mirror, I caught a glimpse of a gorgeous truck driver in tight jeans drinking coffee next to his semi. I reversed into the parking space next to the truck driver and popped up the trunk. I got out and pulled out the Central Valley map. I smiled at the truck driver and was about to ask him directions to Delano when I heard the back window open and my father shout, “Hey, I know where it is. I can tell you.”

I looked away in embarrassment. The truck driver smiled big, and I felt the blood rush to my face. I wondered how my father had read me so well. Had I jerked the car too fast in reverse or had he been watching what I was watching in the side-view mirror? Did he think I wasn’t ever going to get married again?

When I got back into the car, Esteban told me, “You know, I’ve only ever loved one woman . . . only one for me.”

“We’ll have to get out of the car to drink the coffee,” I said to Esteban, ignoring my father. “He doesn’t let anyone drink in his car.”

My father and Esteban stepped out of the car while I went in and bought three coffees. I distributed the cups, the sugars and the creams, and then the three of us drank as we silently looked up at the sky. I wondered what altitude we were at and if being closer to the sky meant we were any closer to our dead loved ones. At any rate, I apologized to my dead husband for looking so ravenously at the truck driver and told him that I missed him.

When I was a kid, I had this beautiful dog. He was a mutt, half Lassie, half shaggy dog. My dog was a car chaser and a sandal robber, and he roamed around wherever and whenever he wanted. My mother called him Diablo, but this was his unofficial name because I had already named him Zeus. Every other kid on the block had a purebred poodle, or Pomeranian, or sheep dog, or Doberman, and all of these dogs were “well trained” and kept inside their homes.

Anyway, Zeus was a great dog and a really smart one too, but he had a bad habit of bringing things home, which got him constantly into trouble. I didn't mind since I was a child, and I thought these were gifts for me.

One day, Zeus decided to pick up all the newspapers in the neighborhood. I thought it was funny when I had to force the patio door open because of the dozen or so *Los Angeles Times* there. But my mother was furious when neighbors started calling, demanding that the dog be walked on a leash. This wasn't really an option since my parents, being Mexican, thought it ridiculous to walk a dog. So my father told me that the only alternatives were to either put the dog to sleep or to find it another home.

I threw myself on the kitchen floor, refused to eat, and begged for mercy, but my father took the dog to the junkyard early the next morning and left him there. Why the junkyard, I don't know. I used to have nightmares about my dog dying of starvation or becoming some other dog, some junkyard beast.

Well, the next day I went berserk and beat the shit out of my next-door neighbor's poodle and the girl who owned it. I threw a newspaper as hard as I could at the poodle and completely knocked the wind out of it. Its head was still jerking back and forth when the owner, a blonde-haired, pastel-dressed Catholic girl, came running at me. I grabbed her by the hair, slugged her a couple of times, and gave her some good scratches on her face. But she was a good fighter and ended up kicking me once in the shins and another time in the stomach.

By the time my mother separated us, we were both a little bloody. Her mother came to our door later that evening and cursed at my mother while I hid behind the dining room table. Her family moved out the following year. My father tried to apologize many times, but they wouldn't have it. He even offered to cut their lawn for free, but they just blew him off.

That's when the Paradas moved in. They became the only other Mexican family on the block. And that's when I first met Nick. He was a pimply foreheaded, bony-shouldered science nerd. He was always talking about his chemistry experiments. His parents confiscated his chemistry set when he burned his bedroom wallpaper.

I would have stayed clear of him, had it not been for his dog. It was a mutt like mine, a wonderful shaggy mutt named Igor. Nick's parents asked my parents about carpooling possibilities, and they convinced my parents to enroll both of us in the same school. That fall we both entered our fifth year at Sacred Heart of Jesus Catholic School. Three years later, at our eighth grade dance, Nick kissed me for the first time. It was an awkward, slimy exchange in which he stuck his tongue in what seemed like the back of my throat. I gagged and then proclaimed I was in love.

We dated through high school, and when we were in our third year of college, he told me, over an In & Out Burger, that if I didn't marry him, he'd lose all hope in life and join the priesthood. That summer we married. When we graduated, we both became high school science teachers. For years we worked, took short vacations, stayed close to our parents, and made vague comments about having children.

The scratchiness of the radio connection decreased as we drove my father's Lincoln Town Car down the Grapevine Highway. Esteban occasionally stroked the dashboard in what I guess was admiration. This is my father's fifth Lincoln Town Car. He purchased the first one in 1967 when he landed his first commercial contract. He started off as a gardener in Beverly Hills, but he worked hard and bought several routes and contracted other Mexicans to do the work for him.

That's when we migrated from East Los Angeles to the suburban town of Arcadia, which my father loves for its neat, little lawns. That's also when my father went from being a gardener to being a landscape artist.

"So tell me, Esteban," my father said, "tell me how they ended up finally kicking you out of town."

"It was an accident. I'm not even sure what I did wrong. One day, Pepe Saguache . . . do you remember Pepe Saguache?"

"Of course," my father replied.

"Well, he died of a heart attack last month."

"Oh, that's too bad. How old was he?"

"He wasn't seventy. He wasn't even sick. Three weeks ago, he told his family he wasn't feeling well and then had an immense heart attack on the way to the outhouse. His sons were so upset that they told me that if they ever saw me around there, they'd kill me. Tomás Saguache, his oldest son, promised to personally slit my throat. What do you think of that, eh, Panchito?"

"But how is it that they blamed you?"

"I don't know," Esteban replied. "I found him soaking his feet in the canal. And I offered him some of my Presidente. We sat there, and he told me that he was ready to divide his six-and-a-half hectares for his sons. He said he'd give each son one hectar and keep one and a half for himself and his wife."

"And that was all?"

"Well, I told him that I met a young man at the sanitarium that had his last name. You know, Saguache is not a common name."

"No, never heard it outside of town."

"The young man, who was also named Pepe Saguache, was from Ojinaga, Chihuahua, where they have cockfights every year. Remember the cockfights?"

"Of course. Do they still have them?"

"No, the arena has long since been torn down. People still go into town in September though. Anyway, this boy, he was not more than fourteen years old, was at the sanitarium because he was born slow. He could never marry, or work, or have kids, and he was constantly trying to kill himself. His mother had committed suicide when he was just a boy. He said that when his grandparents found out that she was pregnant, they threw her out, and she had to make do on the street. She had told them that her godfather had raped her, but her parents hadn't believed her.

"The boy was so depressed that he swore to me that one day he was going to find the son of a bitch who was responsible for bringing him into the world and hang him just like his mother had done to herself. Well, I can't tell you how bad I felt. My heart burned with such compassion and anger that I promised to help him find his father and do justice, if I could.

"Of course, this story affected Pepe. By the time I finished telling him, he had already finished my bottle of Presidente. He got very philosophical about the whole thing."

My father scooted up and grabbed Esteban's shoulder. "Oh my God, Esteban, what did you do?"

"We spoke. That's all. He asked me if a man can be accepted into the glory of heaven if he repents, and so I asked him if he repented, and he said he did. And I told him that was all he could do.

"And then he got all teary eyed and asked if that would get him into heaven. And I told him no. I told him that those who benefit from the pain of others burn in the fires of hell forever—I knew that he believed in that stuff."

"And do you believe that?" my father asked.

"Of course," Esteban said. "You can't undo what's been done. It stays with you forever."

"But that goes against all Christian belief," my father insisted.

"The Church just tells you things you want to hear, so you'll keep going," Esteban said, "and because they want THIS," he said, rubbing his thumb with his index finger.

"That can't be so," my father replied. "So many people who believe, so many people can't be wrong."

"Ay, Panchito, sometimes you amaze me."

I pulled into a gas station at Delano to fill up. My father asked the gas station attendant about an old friend he had in Delano from back in the days when they were hunger striking, but the man couldn't help him, so my father went next door to the mini-market and came back with the address of a man whose name sounded familiar. We drove slowly through paved and unpaved roads leaving a long trail of dust clouds behind us.

My father credits Esteban with saving his life when my father came to the United States for the first time. It was right after World War II, and there was a shortage of men in McAllen, a border town in Texas, so the Pacific Railroad Company put out word that they would hire workers from the Mexican towns near the border. Thousands of men crossed the Rio Grande once the harvest season had ended to work on the railroad tracks.

Well, as soon as my father heard, he snuck across the border because he was madly in love and wanted to marry my mother. He thought he'd work the winter season and be back in early February, but the work was much harder than my father had anticipated.

He and many other men slaved on the tracks all day and then ate and slept in the freight cars. It was really, really cold, and the only place for them to go was a cantina full of *ficheras*, which is one of the many ways to refer to prostitutes in Spanish.

Well, to make a long story short, there was this one *fichera* who was beautiful. Her name was Candela, and my father claims she was absolutely gorgeous. Long, black hair, mango-sized breasts, a small waist, and *pistolera* hips that made your mouth water. My father insists that she was a siren, a true siren, not of this earth. Anyway, this is how my father told it to me.

When I first heard about Candela, I was only nine years old, and I didn't understand a goddamn thing when my father blurted out that a siren had bewitched him.

It was summer, and my mother had let me accompany him. My father was pruning some fancy Caribbean ferns in a beautiful mansion in Hancock Park while I sat on the sidewalk reading a Nancy Drew novel. The owner of the house, a rich Jewish man, would give me a cream puff and a Nancy Drew book every time I'd show up with my father. My father told me he had lost his daughter when she was young in a terrible car accident. Sometimes Mr. Silverstein would help my father water or prune or cover the ferns with a net, because the California sun was a little too intense for them.

They'd spend hours covering the ferns and complaining about their wives. Mr. Silverstein was constantly complaining about his wife refusing to have a baby, and my father would listen intently. That day when my father began to describe Candela's *pistolera* hips, he caught my attention because his voice suddenly got high and he began repeating over and over again what a siren she was. He used the words *sirena* and *el purito Diablo* as if they were synonymous. And then he looked away and sighed, *y pues nos revolcamos en los nopales*, which literally means, well, we rolled around in the cactus (my father's term for having sex), and his eyes got watery.

As I grew older, I understood that my father had fallen for a beautiful prostitute, but she was only interested in the money he was saving for his wedding. When she found the three twenty-dollar bills hidden in his shoe, she stole them.

If that wasn't bad enough, one of the men from my father's hometown (supposedly a friend) went home and told my mother all about Candela. My mother was furious, and she wrote my father that if he didn't get his ass back in town before the Lenten season so they could marry, she was leaving him *y a la chingada* with him, his family, and his *pinche* dreams of *el norte*.

My father claims that the day he received the letter from my mother was the saddest day in his life. He didn't know what to do. He couldn't go home because he didn't have a dime to his name, but he couldn't stay any longer to save up a little because my mother would leave him. So my father sent for Esteban, and when Esteban arrived two weeks later, my father asked him to help him get the money back from Candela.

The cantina was a narrow room with a long bar. The bedrooms were out in the back, in a building behind the cantina. The owner's son, a huge, dim-witted man, guarded the traffic between the cantina and the rooms. The plan was to get past the son and into Candela's room so my father could find the money. Esteban would go into the cantina and dance with her, while my father drank enough tequila with the dim-witted son to get him drunk so he could go into her room and look for the money.

Well, as soon as my father pulled out his bottle of tequila, the dimwit became his best friend. He waited and drank and waited and drank, but the liquor seemed to have little effect on the large man. When my father looked through the cantina window, he saw Esteban slow-dancing with Candela. His eyes were closed, and his arms were wrapped tightly around her. His one hand stroked her long hair, while the other hand sank into her spacious buttocks.

Well, when the dim-witted son finished the bottle and barely burped, my father knew it was over. He was fucked. He'd have no love and no money.

But *La Virgen* was looking out for my father, because as he started to sob and tell the dimwit his sad story, the *migra* arrived out of the blue. Immigration officers in a huge truck and on horseback came charging in. The dim-witted son ran into the cantina, and about fifty men and barmaids ran out with half a dozen immigration officers chasing them into the fields.

Esteban was still dancing with Candela when the immigration officer took her from his arms. My father hid in the shadows of the building and was able to make his way into her room where he found his money nicely wrapped in a girdle.

When they filled their truck with enough *mojados*, the *migra* left. They took Esteban, but my father was able to get away.

Back home, my father bought the wedding rings, the cake, a goat for the meal, and new shoes for himself. Esteban, of course, was my father's best man. The day before the wedding, my father gave Esteban Candela's girdle, which Esteban insisted he would treasure for the rest of his life.

It was at my parents' wedding that Esteban first saw Inés.

"Delano is so quiet," Esteban said. "I think I'll like this place. Will you come and visit me every once in a while?"

"Don't come up here too often," I said.

"When's the last time?" he asked.

"About ten years?" I said as I looked in the rearview mirror and at my father in the back seat. I wasn't sure any more.

"Probably a little longer than that," my father replied. "Nick drove that time."

"Nick is your husband?" Esteban asked me.

"My dead husband," I replied. I looked through the sideview mirror and focused on the utility vehicle behind me that was trying to pass.

"How long has it been?" Esteban asked.

"Five years this November."

Esteban lowered his voice as if he was getting too personal. "Do you dream about him?"

"He's always with my mother in my dreams. I can see them from a distance, but when I try to get close to them, they always send me back," I replied.

"That's because it's not your time. Inés sends me back, too. She tells me to wait it out a few more years."

When Nick started feeling ill at work, we didn't worry too much about it because he had been overworking. But then he started to have to take naps in the car. The pain in his side, he said, was worsening. I took the day off to go with him when the doctor sent him to get X-rays. And when they said they had found a spot on his liver, we were concerned, but not too much. Even when they scheduled the surgery, we thought it impossible that Nick, an otherwise healthy thirty-six-year-old man, could be seriously ill.

On the day of the surgery, I left him early and went to work. He said there was no need for me to be there. He'd be under anesthesia anyway. So I went to work, got out early, and drove to the hospital. There, in front of the elevators, I saw his mother crying. Her head fell into my chest, and she let out a scream. "Not my baby," she said. "Why, God, why!"

The disease had spread everywhere. The doctors said that there was nothing more they could do. They opened him, saw the disaster, and sewed him back up.

That night when Nick awoke, I hugged him for what seemed like forever. I told him to take my energy, that I wanted him to have it, that he should hold on to me for everything, that through some transcendence I was giving him all of my healthy cells, and if human desire can alter the world, then I could alter the reality of our hospital room. He would not die, I told him, because I wouldn't let him. I said it with such fierceness and adrenaline that I think for a moment he believed me. "Right on," he said. "That's my girl." But he died a week later anyway.

At the funeral, my godmother, sensing my anger and confusion, told me that I should consider myself lucky to have had that last week with Nick. "It's a blessing to be able to tie up the loose ends. Some people lose their loved ones in an instant," she said to me. I took a long, good look at her and wondered if I should tell her what I felt, that she was a self-righteous bitch, an insensitive fuck who still had her husband and four daughters. But I just burst into tears. What do you do when your future is reduced to one week? What do you say? I told him I loved him. He told me he loved me. I told him I was scared. He said he was too. I told him I wouldn't know how to go on. He told me I had to try. It seems ridiculous to me now how our speech became stupidly simplistic and deliberate.

Months later, I realized that my dialogue with him was not over. It couldn't be over. I still had too many questions. Even if I had to invent his answers, these dialogues would continue in my head.

We had dinner at a Denny's in Delano. After my father ate his lemon meringue pie, he took out from his shirt pocket a crumpled phone bill envelope where he kept a list of all the places Esteban might find a place to stay. He had already crossed out four of the five names of people who were already dead or in rest homes or had gone back to Mexico.

"Well, I have one more name," my father said. "It's with the town priest."

"I don't want to stay with a priest," Esteban replied. "They give me the willies."

"He's a good man. You'll see," my father replied. "I just hope we can find him."

"Leave me on the outskirts of town," Esteban said.

"There's nothing out there," my father replied.

"The fields are out there," Esteban replied.

My father shook his head in disapproval. He looked at me, but I didn't know what to say. Esteban reached his hand over to my father and pressed against my father's wrist. "I don't know how to repay you, Panchito."

As we drove to the edge of town, Esteban said, "I'll tell you when to stop." It was dark as we drove alongside groves of peach trees. The moon was full and bright. Minutes passed before Esteban said, "Right here."

Esteban got out of the car with a sack of Denny's leftovers. My father jumped out of the car with him and gave him a backpack with a first-aid packet, Nick's denim shirts, a throw blanket, and a jacket he had in the back seat. Then he reached for his wallet and pulled out the bills he had in there. He even searched deep into his front pockets and gave him his change.

"Wait," my father replied. "Write down my phone number on this," he said as he gave me the crumpled envelope paper.

When I handed it to Esteban, he winked his eye and said, "Don't forget to visit me." I reached out to shake his hand.

My father told him, "If you can't make a go of it here, listen to your instincts and go home. You're too old for these boyhood adventures." My father held out his hand, but Esteban pushed it away and grabbed him close in a tight embrace. Then Esteban walked right into the groves of peach trees. With the car light, we were able to see him for a hundred feet or so, but then he just disappeared into the darkness.

My father stood in front of the car with his hands on his hips, staring at the darkness Esteban had walked into. He turned to me, the lights in his face, and just lifted his hands. Then he walked to the driver's door. I slid over to make room for him. He was still shaking his head as he adjusted the mirrors and the seat, and then he took off fast.

We stopped again in Gorman on our way back to get a cup of coffee so we wouldn't fall asleep. "So whatever happened to Inés's head?" I asked.

"It's too terrible to talk about," he said.

"Tell me anyway," I said.

He frowned. "When Inés's head disappeared, everyone thought it was *brujería*, that Esteban was practicing black magic and that he had paid someone to steal the head. In any case, the *sargento* was so pissed off about the whole thing that he was threatening to pistol-whip a confession out of Esteban. When they pistol-whip you, they can easily kill you. I knew that Esteban wasn't into black magic, so I went to the judge to ask him about the missing head. His wife was there, and she kept speaking for him, insisting that they knew nothing more about it. Her insistence made me suspicious. I told them that if Esteban was pistol-whipped to death, his soul would be restless and come back to torture them. That was enough to get a confession out of the judge's hideous wife.

"She said that with all the moving around, Inés's head had completely torn away from the body and fell off the table. And because the judge had forgotten to close the barn door, their pig had come in and had mistaken Inés's head for food. She had nibbled on the head so much that Inés's face was unrecognizable. The judge and his wife didn't know how to explain this to Inés's family and the rest of the town, so they let the rumors about *brujería* spread. The judge's wife confessed to me that she buried Inés's head by their stable because she couldn't think of anything else to do with it. So I went and told the *sargento* the story, *en confianza*, and Esteban's life was spared."

"So Inés's head is buried next to a stable full of pigs?" I said in disbelief.

"Probably not a stable anymore," my father replied. "You know how things change."

There was nothing more to say after that. My father switched on the cruise control and clicked on the radio to one of his Spanish stations. It was the Saturday night *corrido* hour, and we heard a ballad about two men in a bar confessing to each other their sad love stories only to find out that they were in love with the same woman.

And then we heard another ballad about a brave revolutionary who prays to *La Virgen* to care for his mother as he faces execution. And then another one about a jilted husband who kills his wife and burns his house down with green firewood because green wood burns faster. The moon was a bright, yellowish white.

When I had heard enough, I turned away and created a story of my own. It was a story about a woman who was in love with her dead husband, a woman who refused to believe he was dead. In her story, the woman drives through endless freeways at night, her heart like a moving headlight, illuminating every overpass and offramp making sure she didn't miss a single inch of the many miles that she had traveled in her search for him. There was no murder, no guilt, and few regrets, and yet there was an underlying madness to find him, her need to feel him there, body and spirit, once more.

The Red Curtain

There's a huge nuclear power plant in San Diego. You can see it as you drive south on Interstate 5. Two white domes, very round. Somehow, I thought, quite feminine. I told my brother Andy, who was driving, about how feminine the domes were. Andy is a twenty-nine-year-old seismologist in San Francisco, quite handsome and charming in an understated way. And I'm not just saying that because he's my brother.

Andy agreed that the roundness of the plants had a certain voluptuousness, a certain curvaceousness that suggested femininity. He said this with a smile.

We both went to Cal, but I dropped out when I was a junior and returned to Los Angeles to pursue my art. Mostly I worked on installations because they showed how fragmented my life had been, pieces from here and there that didn't quite fit together. I'd had a few art shows, but none of them successful (it's hard to sell a twenty-foot installation), so I was working as a bus driver during the day. I drove the small buses, those buses for "special needs" kids. That's where I met Richard.

My husband Richard, who insisted on coming along, said that only *I* could come up with such an insane idea as a power plant being feminine. I reminded him that the word "plant" in Spanish is *planta* and that in Spanish it *is* feminine.

My husband annoyed me. He'd annoyed me for some time now, probably years, but the bickering had recently gotten meaner, more aggressive. As long as I was in the car with Andy, though, I was determined to control myself. I didn't want my brother to feel uncomfortable. Things were difficult enough for us having to take this trip and scatter our mother's ashes into the Pacific Ocean.

It was with quiet acceptance that we saw our mother pass three weeks ago. She had been battling cancer for seven years. Seven horrible years of seeing her suffer. But it did give her enough time to resolve things, to tie up loose ends with us. If she was scared, she didn't show it.

She whispered to me, in careful details, her past. In her elliptical way, she spoke of her true love, of the real reason she left Mexico over thirty years ago. When it was time, she told me, I should share these stories with Andy.

Andy stopped at a rest area in Oceanside and sprawled a huge map of Baja on top of our car. We would pick a cliff in Mexico nearest the border, he said, pointing to several spots that might be suitable.

Our mother had requested that her ashes be scattered at the border, somewhere between San Diego and Ensenada. Because her heart belonged in both countries and ultimately in neither, the ashes should go into the ocean. So Andy and I were intent on finding the "right" place for her ashes.

With a pencil, Andy carefully calculated the distance from the border of the most suitable spot. "There are some cliffs thirty miles south of the border," he said. "Would Mom have considered that close enough?" he asked me. "I can't tell what direction the wind is blowing. What if it's blowing south?"

"Instead of throwing the ashes off a cliff, we could rent a boat and throw them directly into the sea? I think that might be better."

"You're right. But we won't be able to get that close to the border," he said. "I'm sure the Border Patrol doesn't allow it."

"We'll get as close as we can get."

Once we approached the border, I tensed up. As soon as I saw the Mexican soldier standing stiffly at the border in his green fatigues and a machine gun in his hand, I told Richard to take the urn off the seat and place it carefully on the floor of the car. "It's just a vase," he said. "How the hell would they know what's inside?"

"Just do it," I said.

Andy looked nervous driving his new SUV in Tijuana. People cut in front of him and honked because he was driving too slow. We couldn't see any signs that pointed toward the beaches. "I don't want to get lost," he said softly. "I'd rather go slow than get lost."

"Drive any slower, Andy, and you might get us killed," Richard said.

I turned back and gave him a dirty look. "Do you want me to drive?" I asked Andy.

"I'm okay. I think we're headed toward the beaches."

A brothel town in northern Mexico, 1965

An adobe wall enclosed the brothel town. Instead of walking through the main entrance, Chata walked around it until she came up to a part of the wall that had completely collapsed and then stepped over carefully. She had on *vaquero* boots, jeans, and a white cowboy shirt with shiny buttons. A grey cowboy hat covered most of her face.

Dusk was setting in. She watched the men as they came in and out of the brothels and cantinas and reflected sadly on her predicament.

Of all the women in her family, she was the only gay one. No one knew, of course. Hers was the life of the spinstered *maestra*, a woman more interested in books than men, at least that was how her mother explained it.

She sighed as she began to wipe the dust from her boots and jeans. She wanted so much to appear beautiful to Socorro, a prostitute who worked at El Farolito, a brothel with a hacienda-style courtyard. The patio was beautiful, full of roses and fruit trees that were cared for by the barmaids. The place was owned by Don Maximiliano Saavedra, a Spaniard from Zaragoza whose family had returned to Spain after losing everything to the Revolution. But he stayed and grew fat waiting for the land to be returned to him.

Chata snuck in through the service entrance. She climbed the wooden stairs and leaned against the stucco walls, her body in the shadow of the stairwell. She knocked gently. Socorro, who was dressed only in a black slip, greeted her with an exuberant kiss. Her breasts were small and firm and fit perfectly in the cup of the slip. It clung to her and looked very sexy. But she didn't look well. There were bags underneath her eyes, and her bangs hung limply to one side.

"Did Don Maximiliano see you?" asked Socorro.

"Maybe. I don't know if he's ever seen me."

"He's seen you all right. Not your face, but he's seen you. I told him we were lovers. True lovers. But he still wants to start charging you."

"He can go fuck himself."

Chata smiled and kissed Socorro firmly. Her mouth opened, and she took in Socorro's tongue as she played with her auburn hair, caressing the back of her neck, gently pulling the short, thin hairs there, and then gently stroking the upper part of her back. Socorro returned the neck kisses and softly bit the lower lobe of Chata's ear. Chata lost herself in Socorro's touch and closed her eyes.

Socorro's parents had been murdered when she was seven. When her father had claimed his right to irrigate his land with water from the canal, the larger landowners refused to share the water with him. He, of course, fought them at the town meeting, called them *una bola de bandidos* and *unos sin vergüenzas, hijos de sus chingadas madres.*

When the meeting was finished, they gunned him down as he was crossing the plaza. Socorro's mother ran into the plaza thinking she could save him, that they wouldn't dare shoot a woman, but they gunned her down, too.

The bodies lay on the dirt in the middle of the plaza for hours because no one dared try to remove them. Chata remembered how the dead woman's hand clasped the man's shirt, how the look on her face was one of complete disbelief, how the small pool of blood formed beneath her open mouth.

But more than anything, Chata remembered Socorro screaming and kicking the dirt. Don Pedro, a kind old man and the plaza caretaker, picked her up, carried her on his hips, and handed her over to the town priest where she stayed for the next eight years of her life.

Some of Chata's earliest memories were of her and Socorro playing dolls in the room behind the sacristy. When they felt mischievous, they'd borrow robes and candles from the sacristy and baptize each other's dolls, which made them their doll's godparents.

No one ever volunteered to care for Socorro, and when she turned fifteen, she ran away. It was never explained why, but the priest grieved greatly, and the townspeople said the grieving was excessive and unnatural. Chata also grieved Socorro's leaving, but no one bothered commenting about it.

Socorro roamed the streets for a while, taking a house-cleaning job, then a waitressing job, and occasionally wrote Chata and told her where she was. It didn't matter if she did, since there was no way that Chata could visit her. Her tyrannical mother wouldn't allow it.

Three years later, Socorro took up residence in the brothel. When Chata heard, she was devastated. She wrote Socorro a long, confused letter asking her to leave the brothel, to leave town, to leave with her, but Socorro was unashamed. Even smug about it. "It's just my body," she wrote Chata back.

Chata was furious when she read Socorro's response, so furious that she got the courage to visit Socorro at the brothel for the first time, and that's when the romance began. In a passionate plea that Socorro leave the brothel, Chata had clumsily confessed her love for her.

For two years now, Chata had escaped from her mother, and her miserable existence as a schoolteacher, and into Socorro's bedroom in the city's legalized whore town.

Chata opened her eyes and stared at the bright, tacky flowers on the walls. The turning ventilator dizzied her with its slow circular movement. She saw the brass bed headboard and began thinking of those fathers who paid so that Socorro would give their sons "experience." Boys who would ejaculate in their pants. Older men that Socorro would have to play with endlessly to get an ejaculation. And all those men that had ejaculated in her, on her stomach, in her mouth, on her breasts, and on and on, and it created an incredible disgust, a repulsion, and a rage—a contained rage that was torturing Chata.

She felt Socorro's hand on her knee and then felt her lips kiss her shoulder. She pulled her shoulder in, away from Socorro. Both lay in bed in silence.

"Let's leave," Chata said as though she was gasping for air.

Socorro remained silent.

"I need you to leave this place!" insisted Chata.

"And you'd pay my rent?" Socorro responded angrily.

"I'd do anything for you," replied Chata.

"Pay the rent," she taunted.

"I can't take this anymore!" Chata yelled and then controlled herself. "That's all I feel." She paused and turned to face Socorro. "Let's leave, let's go to Ciudad Juarez. Or we can cross the *río* to El Paso. There, no one will know. And we'll look for work. As long as one of us is working."

"Doing what?"

"What does it matter? Any work. Cleaning houses, waiting tables, washing dishes, working in the fields. It doesn't matter to me. I just want to be with you."

Socorro kissed Chata softly. She kept her cheek next to Chata's so that Chata thought for a moment that Socorro was really listening to her. But then Socorro said quietly, "You need to leave in a little while."

Chata pulled away. She had grown suspicious of Socorro. Perhaps Socorro liked her lifestyle, enjoyed all these sexual antics, the constant fornication. And she thought Socorro was lazy. She'd rather lie on her back than pick corn, or cotton, or clean houses. She had grown used to the compromises. And she thought Socorro was vain. Socorro was quite aware of her beauty. She knew that men lusted after the roundness of her breasts and hips, the smoothness of her skin, the shine of her reddish-brown hair. Men wanted to satisfy that profound yearning she had in her sad, brown eyes.

Chata turned. "I'm going to stay tonight. I'm going to see you dance," she said.

"You're crazy," Socorro snapped.

Chata sat up. An incredible jealousy overcame her—an usurping emotion unlike ever before that prompted her to grab Socorro by the arms and shake her violently. Socorro grabbed Chata's hands as she tried to pull away. Chata slapped her. "You dance for them. Now dance for me! Dance for me now!"

After she said it, Chata looked for apologetic words to come out, but she couldn't find them. She wasn't sorry. She was tired of it all.

Socorro got up and turned on her phonograph. She let her slip fall to the floor and began to dance naked and barefoot in front of Chata. She twirled slowly and lifted her hands as though she danced with a partner. She bowed back in slow dips.

Chata stared at the beauty of Socorro's movements. Socorro was like a nymph, like an angel—ephemeral, translucent. Chata was consumed with awe. Then despair set in. She realized the transparency of both their lives. The intangibility of their happiness, the precociousness of her dream. It was so incredibly absurd and cruel that she began sobbing.

Socorro wrapped her arms around Chata, wiped her tears with her hands. She stroked her hair until Chata stopped sobbing and then took in the warmth of her breath, consumed it, let it enter the abyss in her heart.

"Señorita Socorro, the band is ready. We go on in half an hour or so," a voice said from beyond the door.

"I'll be out soon," replied Socorro as she got up and grabbed her slip from the ground.

Socorro stood in front of the dresser mirror and applied cheap, creamy-pink eye shadow and deep red lipstick. She put on a bright green, velour blouse that showed her black bra. Her skirt was dark and tight and high cut in the back.

She opened the door and shouted down the hallway, "I'm ready."

The water was choppy, so I hung onto the urn tightly. The small boat jolted to and fro, and I felt like crying, but I didn't want the floodgate of emotion to burst open, so I thought about happy times. I thought about me resting my head on my mother's chest when we watched Spanish soap operas together. I was still living with her then.

Our favorite soap was a Venezuelan one that followed the love lives of three beautiful Amazonian sisters. Mother insisted that she could saddle, ride, and hunt better than the three sisters put together. I teased her, called her the Mexican Spitfire, insisted that she was exaggerating, that she was pulling my leg, but I sensed then that there was a lot about my mother I didn't know. Her touch had magic. As soon as I placed my head on her lap or shoulder or chest, I felt a comfort deep inside of me.

The wind slapped against my face. The immensity of the ocean was scary. Is this what Mother would have wanted, for us to surrender her to this immensity? I'd feel so lost. It tortured me to think that I was surrendering her to this vastness. A part of me wanted to jump in with her, if only to keep her company. I turned and looked at Andy. He was crying. His Cal baseball cap and his sunglasses covered most of his face, but somehow I still knew he was crying.

When the boat engine stopped, Andy took the urn from me. "I'll do it," he said.

"Say something," I said to him.

"Words can't express what I feel," he replied. "Which way is the wind blowing?"

"That way," I said.

He walked to the bow of the boat, raised the urn, and then carefully turned it over. The wind took the ashes before most of them could reach the ocean water.

Richard sat sullenly away from us for the entire boat ride. I was glad that he hadn't gotten involved, that he had been respectfully low-key. He had loved my mother, too, I guess. As much as Richard can love anyone.

When Mother first found out that she had cancer, she told me repeatedly how much she didn't want me to be alone, that a companion was necessary. She didn't have to tell me that. The thought of being without her caused me such dread that I married Richard without being in love with him. That was my fault.

He was handsome and attentive and interested in my artwork, but he wasn't imaginative or passionate. And he was unfaithful. I knew, but I told myself that I didn't care. I couldn't care. Mom was sick, and then there was my artwork.

The crowd was waiting for her. Boisterous, irreverent. Socorro walked in seductively, teasing the men by touching their hands, the backs of their heads. She paraded toward the bar where the musicians waited for her. The accordionist began singing, and she joined in when the pitch wasn't too high. They sang one song after another and received a loud applause each time. The crowd demanded more.

A mustached man, tall, paunchy, and rude, came up to her and hugged her aggressively. Then everyone began clapping and the same man slapped his hand on the table and said, "Here! Dance here!"

"I'll fall, Pedro," said Socorro pleadingly.

"I'll catch you, of course, Socorro," he replied.

"I didn't say the music should stop," he yelled to the musicians.

The table was wet and uneven, and Socorro's heels were so old that the metal wore through the leather, and that made it all the more slippery for her. As soon as she stepped on the table, she almost fell. She sang off-key, but she still looked beautiful.

She knew Pedro Fuentes well. He was rough and abrupt, even cruel. And yet quite charming. Most of the barmaids thought him handsome. So virile. They envied Socorro. He could sleep with the blonde women in the brothel down the street, for instance, but every time he came to town, he'd come to see Socorro. Everyone accepted his respectability. He was rich. That was all, and that was everything.

Pedro Fuentes was also Chata's uncle. Socorro had never told Chata that she had slept with him. There was no need to cause more pain. Chata was so proud. In some ways, Chata was as righteous and as proper and as close-minded as her mother.

Chata lay in bed waiting for Socorro to finish singing. She could hear the distant shouts. To block them out, she thought about Ciudad Juarez, about El Paso, about the hustle and bustle of a *frontera* town. What would it be like to get lost in it with Socorro? They would leave next Sunday, on All Soul's Day, when going to the brothel was restricted and when her mother would be visiting relatives in Zacatecas.

Then Chata heard Socorro's shouts. Chata raced down the hallway to the red cloth that draped the doorway to the bar. She swung the drape open, but then hid behind the wall's shadow.

"Get that drunk away from me!" Socorro yelled from behind the bar. Pedro Fuentes looked furious. In his hand, he held the neck of a broken beer bottle. The jagged edge of the green glass shone as he swung it around him, so that no one dared approach him.

Pedro slurred as he said to Don Maximiliano, "How much for that one?"

Don Maximiliano took out his revolver from underneath the bar and placed it on the bar, so Pedro could see it. Don Maximiliano had earned the reputation of being fierce when provoked.

"Don Pedro, the señorita doesn't want to dance with you. Pick any of the other girls. Drop the bottle and let me get you something to eat."

"I'm not hungry," Pedro replied.

"Put the glass down and sit down or leave, Don Pedro."

"Or what?"

Don Maximiliano's hazel eyes blazed, but he spoke calmly as he placed his hand on the revolver. "If I shoot you it would cause an unfortunate scandal, and that would be bad for business."

Pedro Fuentes slammed the bottle on the floor, shattering it into pieces, and reached for his pocket. Don Maximiliano seized the revolver and pointed it at Don Pedro's chest. Don Pedro jerked his hands up. "My wallet," he said.

Chata watched the entire scene from the curtain folds. She threw her head back, banging it against the wall as if in disbelief. How could Socorro sleep with her uncle? How humiliating love is, she thought. How devoid of dignity. She heard the clacking of Socorro's heels coming toward her. She hid in the shadows when she heard Don Maximiliano's voice.

"And where do you think you're going?" he said.

"I don't want to," replied Socorro.

"He's offered three hundred. You can take half. You don't make that in a year," he said.

"I don't care. He's a pig."

"Socorro, we're all pigs."

"I don't care," she insisted.

"And who the hell are you not to care? Take it."

"No," shouted Socorro.

"I've already taken my cut," he said. "If he slits your throat, I'll take yours too," he said as he walked away.

"I want to stay by the shore," Andy said. "Take the car and go eat. I want to be alone."

Andy had recently converted to Buddhism. He said it gave him peace of mind, that it had helped him through Mom's illness. Surprisingly, Mother did not mind at all that he had changed religions. She wasn't religious at all. "You're Mexican, so I guess you're Catholic," she would say halfheartedly those two or three times she walked us to church.

Richard drove around Ensenada looking for a decent place to eat. We parked and walked down a busy street full of bars, nightclubs, and restaurants, but I didn't want to go into any of them. They were full of boisterous young people, obnoxious American soldiers, drunken white people who had forgotten their manners when they crossed the border. "Get me out of here," I said to Richard.

We drove farther into town, past pockets of residential areas. We drove around and around. "Just stop at the nearest taco stand," I said to him.

"I want a decent meal," he said. "I want to eat at a restaurant."

"At the rate we're going, we're not going to eat at all," I snapped.

Richard parked the car abruptly and stared at me. "We need to talk when we get back," he said.

"Well, talk," I replied.

"Not now."

"Right now," I insisted.

He sighed and said, "I know it's not a good time, but I have to tell you something."

I looked at him angrily. But inside I felt more dread than anger. I sensed what was coming. "What is it then?" I said to him.

"I'm . . . " he said and then turned away. "I've fallen in love. I'm sorry. I don't know how it happened."

"Do I know her?"

"Yes."

"Is it Susan?"

"Yes," he replied.

"You're such a bastard. Such an insensitive bastard!" I said as I ran out of the car. Richard followed me in the car, block after block.

To get away from him, I walked into a club, through its empty dance floor, and out the back door and into the alley. It was very seedy. I saw a cantina not far from where I was, and I walked to it. As I approached it, I heard *norteño* music, my mother's music, coming from inside. The entrance was open, and I walked into a short, narrow hallway and to a thick red plastic curtain.

Beyond the curtain, I could hear accordions. I slowly moved the plastic curtain to one side and looked in. The room was full of men. Several waitresses in leotard tops and short shorts and heels walked around serving them. I pressed my arm against my purse. Common sense told me to walk away. Of course, I didn't.

The bartender, a good-looking woman with high cheekbones and fake blonde hair, looked at me as I walked to the bar and sat down. She raised her eyebrows, asking what I wanted to drink.

"A beer," I said in Spanish.

"What kind?" the woman said. I stared at her blankly. I thought about Susan Miller, the bimbo, the airhead dispatcher with the huge gap between her front teeth. Of all the women at work, he had to pick the stupidest one.

"What kind of beer?"

"Tecate," I responded.

She looked at me inquisitively. "Are you looking for someone?"

"My husband," I said. "My husband just left me." The pain was in my voice. "He left me for an idiot." My Spanish was broken and that embarrassed me because I looked Mexican. People at work and on the streets would speak to me in Spanish, but Mom had never taught me Spanish. When I asked, she'd always reply, "What for?" But I still felt ashamed, so a couple of years ago, I started taking Spanish classes. I told myself I was doing it to help the mothers of the kids I drove every day. In exchange for a happy-face sticker, Esmeralda, a beautiful nine-year-old girl with Down syndrome, would teach me one Spanish word on the bus ride to school. Her mother was completely illiterate and was beaten regularly by her husband. I would see the bruises on her arms, sometimes on her face, and the terrible sadness, a disconnection, in her eyes. A part of me thought that if I was kind to this woman and child every day, then God would have mercy on my own miserable existence.

"It's still early," the bartender replied. "People start arriving after eleven. But don't sit here. Take the back booth." She pointed to the last booth in the bar. "If you sit there, you can see everyone who comes and goes. At any rate, men won't confuse you for one of the girls." She paused. "I hope you find what you're looking for."

The girls, I presumed, were the prostitutes hanging out at the other end of the bar.

"Why haven't you left? You should have left when I told you!" Socorro screamed at Chata.

"Please tell me you haven't been with him," Chata begged. "Please tell me that."

"Why hurt you with this?" Socorro replied dejectedly. "I do what I do. Makes no difference what man it is. He's willing to pay one hundred and fifty. That's enough to get us to El Paso. We could go—like you said."

Socorro tried kissing Chata, holding her close, leaning her head into Chata's neck, but Chata pushed her away. "No!"

Don Maximiliano stepped into the hallway when he heard them arguing. Chata's back was to him, but she could see his shadow against the white stuccoed wall of the stairway. Socorro pushed her hand forward in a weak wave as if to tell him everything was all right. The shadow disappeared.

"There's no time, Chata, I have to go," Socorro said as she walked quickly down the stairs, then down the hallway past the red curtain.

Enraged, Chata felt an impulse to grab Socorro and drag her out if she had to. Instead, she followed her down the stairs and hallway, but stopped at the red curtain again. It might as well have been a brick wall.

Chata sobbed as she walked out the service entrance. She was consumed by the impossibility of it all. There wasn't a place here where they could be happy together. It was only with Socorro that she had ever felt joy—glimpses here and there—for hours at a time. Perhaps it was just the rush of anticipation, not happiness that she felt with her. And what would happen if the townspeople found out about her and Socorro? She had heard of lesbians being beaten or gang raped. Her mother, cold and pretentious as she was, would certainly disown her. Was Socorro worth this? A part of her knew she should go home, like Socorro said, but adrenaline kept her there, standing behind the brothel, kicking the dirt with her boots. Then Chata saw the light in Socorro's room turn on.

Chata ran back inside the brothel up the stairs. She caught her breath as she turned the knob slowly. Socorro was face down. Her eyes were open wide and fixed on the wall in front of her. They were empty.

Pedro plunged into Socorro. Her left palm pushed into the mattress as if to control his thrusting body. Pedro's cross flew frantically in the air. Drops of sweat fell from his chin. He was so consumed by his thrusting and panting that he didn't notice Chata in the room.

Without thinking, Chata took the fat vase full of water and yellow roses and with all her might swung it at Pedro. It crashed against his neck and the back of his head, and he fell forward unconscious. Socorro cringed back in fear, but she didn't scream.

She jumped up and began pulling Chata away from the bed. "Chata, leave . . . Chata, leave," she said ten times, but Chata froze at the sight of her uncle passed out on the bed. There was a growing stain of blood on the sheets. A yellow rose lay on his bare skin. "Please, God help me, Chata, you have to go," she pleaded.

She grabbed her slip and put it on. She pulled Chata up from the bed, walked her toward the door, and then carefully down the stairs, telling her that everything would be all right. Walked her to the adobe wall that separated the brothel town from the rest of the world. "Go," she told her. But Chata just stood there. "I beg you, please go," she said as she pushed her away. "For that part of you that loves me, please go . . . may God hear me." Chata began to sob. Socorro started pounding her fist into Chata. "Go, goddamn it. You fucking bitch, go!" Socorro turned and ran back into the brothel. Chata heard the door slam.

Chata felt as though she were in a daze. Her body felt foreign, as if she didn't fit into it. As she started walking, she thought of the first time she kissed Socorro. A butterfly kiss that made her dizzy. The fluttering of her eyelashes against Socorro's cheek. She was having a hard time remembering all the details. Where was she when she did it? And did Socorro respond by confessing her love? Perhaps that was later. Yes, maybe when she kissed her passionately on the mouth. Fragments of memory came to her lethargically, vaguely. She quickened her step. Socorro was far, far away. Too far. What should she do? She touched her temple. "My God, how tired I am! How incredibly tired."

"Do you sell cigarettes?" I asked the waitress.

"I sell a lot of things," she smiled mischievously at me. It made me nervous, and I looked away.

She came back five minutes later with another beer and a cigarette next to it on her tray. "This one is on me," she said.

I took it and thanked her as she lit the cigarette for me. She was a thin woman with large breasts. They sagged enough for me to conclude that they were real. She stared at my wedding band and then gave me that smile again.

"I guess you're used to seeing people come in here all the time who've made that mistake," I said.

"And what mistake would that be?" she asked.

"The mistake of getting married," I replied.

"All the time," she said as she walked away. I was on my fourth beer and was starting to feel quite drunk. I didn't know how I was going to get to the hotel, and I had little cash left.

The cantina was full of Mexican men, most of them in their work clothes. A group of them sat huddled in front of me as they cracked jokes, at times laughing so hard that they'd slump over in their chairs or slap their hands on their knee or on the table. I could tell they were talking about me, daring each other to approach me. One of them called over the musicians, and I saw him take out his wallet and hand over several bills.

The musicians, an accordionist, a bass player, and a guitarist, moved in my direction. The accordionist asked me if there was anything special I'd like to hear. I said no. I didn't know any songs by name and I wasn't about to tell him that. The musicians wore ugly dark-green polyester suits with black cowbow hats.

I always have enjoyed the accordion, and the musician played it very well. The song was about a woman's beautiful dark eyes. The guitarist also played very well, but I was a bit dismayed by the bass player who simply seemed to pluck one string and then the other to create the steady omm-pau-pau sound that all *norteño* music seems to have as a backbeat. The bass player, a huge beer-bellied man, had a cowhide belt buckle with his initials: G.O.D. I imagined it was Guillermo Ordoñez Díaz or Gilberto Omar Dávila or something like that.

The accordionist sang with such yearning that I inevitably thought of my mother, and my eyes grew watery. How I needed her right now. I puckered my lips, trying to contain my pain. Of all the places to be on this night, I had chosen a dive in the seedy part of Ensenada, motherless, husbandless, and facing G.O.D. It was so pathetic I couldn't help laughing at myself. Was the fat, hairy fucker in front of me an angel in disguise? Some godsend to help me cross this bridge in my life?

As divergent as my mother's world had been from mine, she had been in a place like this. She had fallen in and out of love in a bar just like this one. I wondered if my future held a trip, a longer trip, into Mexico, into a brothel town in search of the woman my mother once loved. I could only imagine what her mother had gone through. Her being gay surprised me, sure, but what surprised me most was my mother's passion, her intensity, her maddening love for this woman. I wasn't sure there was a need to go and search out what I now knew.

My mother's lover was inconsequential. People fall in and out of love all the time. What mattered was that Mom had the courage to reinvent herself, to create a new life for herself in another country, alone. How more courageous can one be?

I never got the guts to ask Mom if we were her biological children. I don't suppose it matters. I am, regardless of genetics, her daughter, and this is her legacy.

By this time, I was feeling quite drunk. A rather handsome man from the group of men in front of me had slid into my booth. Another beer was placed on the table for me. Every time he smiled, his large, ripe Adam's apple would move. He had wonderful dark skin.

This man, I don't think he introduced himself by name, touched my hand and then gently urged me out of the booth to dance with him. I hesitated because I had never danced to *norteño* music before, but I gave in. He touched me gently on my hips and slowly showed me his movements. His gyrations matched the beat perfectly. They were paced and although contained, very sexy. I tried following him as best I could. As the beat of the music quickened, so did he. I did my best to follow him. And I felt great. I felt Mexican. I felt close to Mom. I felt liberated. My hips were moving and my arms were spread. I would have probably started taking off my blouse if a gentle hand hadn't pulled me from the crowd. It was my brother Andy.

I rested my head on his shoulder. His hand pressed against my cheek. "Don't ever leave me like that, okay?" he said. "I don't know what I'd do if you left me too," he said, his voice breaking. "I've been looking for you like mad for the last six hours. Let's go home."

As soon as I got into his car, I fell asleep. I didn't open my eyes again until we were in Irvine. Andy stopped at a donut shop to get a cup of coffee. The seat was as far back as it could go. I was lying on my side. Andy cleared the hair in my face and asked me if I wanted anything. "Just water," I said.

"Richard said he'd find his own way home," he said.

"What else did he tell you?" I asked.

"Said the two of you were breaking up."

"He's leaving me for another woman."

"Let him go. He doesn't deserve you. You know, you should come up and stay with me. We could spend some time together like we used to."

"Your apartment is tiny."

"Not any smaller than the room we grew up in."

"What about your love life?"

"You're not staying with me permanently," he smiled. "Let me buy a big cup of coffee. We'll stop at your place, just long enough for you to pack a suitcase of clothes, and then we'll drive straight to San Francisco."

"What about my job?"

"You can be a bus driver anywhere. Don't you have some artwork to do?"

I told him that for my next installation I wanted to work with cloth, red cloth. Red cloth suspended or hanging in succession somehow. And these pieces of cloth would hide white domes made out of paper. I told him I wanted to use light, that Frankenstein kind of light that moves up and down, to penetrate the red cloth. And I wanted to use the strings of a bass or a guitar to hang these pieces of cloth. Andy listened to me intently as I struggled to describe what I wanted.

When I finished, he smiled and told me I shouldn't worry about getting a job in San Francisco. If there wasn't a bus driver position available, I could always work as a dancer in the Tenderloin. I told him he said that because he was jealous. He said he absolutely was jealous. He was jealous that I had inherited Mom's dancing gene.

I told him that a year from now, on the anniversary of her death, we should go dancing to celebrate her, to remember what a vivacious, intense person she was. Our grieving was so strong, and those happy moments with her seemed so distant.

We needed to tell each other these stories, I insisted, to save us from despair. He said we should start right now, and he began to tell me about the time he caught Mom dancing in front of her closet mirror. She got so mad she chased him around the apartment with a broom.

We caught morning traffic on Interstate 5 as we approached Los Angeles. The downtown skyscrapers were barely visible through the thick clouds of smog. It would be another forty minutes before we'd reach my Hollywood apartment. There was no doubt in my mind or in my heart that Andy could handle Mother's past. In time, I would tell him, in every precious detail, in the same elliptical way and with the same *telenovela* drama, the story of our mother's first true love.

The Swap Meet

It was eleven o'clock at the Starlight Swap Meet and sales sucked. Stevie was a part-time plumber who sold on Sundays to drum up enough money for the rent. At least that's what he told his wife, Esmeralda. She demanded a check for every plumbing job he did. She even kept a log.

Esmeralda said she had to keep track of everything on account of Stevie's drinking problem. According to him, it was because she was a power-tripping bitch. Still, it was much easier for him to pocket the swap meet profits. At the very least it bought him his week's supply of beer and a carton of cigarettes.

The truth is Esmeralda hated Stevie. She was beautiful and shrewd and utterly convinced that she had married a loser. She knew it a long time ago, but she stayed because she didn't have anywhere else to go. Stevie met her when she was still a factory worker in need of papers, so she married him. But it was never love. She had considered leaving him many times, of going back to Mexico, but she had too much pride to return to her hometown alone.

Esmeralda hated the swap meet too, but it was a habit. Like church. And she had grown accustomed to seeing the vendors every week. Especially one vendor. For the last six months, she had had a lover. A handsome, virile, younger man who made her feel alive again.

This morning, like many Sunday mornings before, Esmeralda had made an excuse to spend time with her lover. She had left her son Penguin asleep on the truck bed and had gone to the other end of the swap meet to drink coffee and exchange subtle affections with him. The longing looks, the holding of hands underneath the table, the way he touched her knee. These were hours of foreplay for her, and they intensified her desire for the lovemaking they reserved for weekday afternoons, when Stevie had his plumbing jobs and Penguin was in school.

Only recently had they become careless. One of her regular customers saw them drinking coffee from the same cup, and he gave her a dirty look. Another vendor saw them exchanging romantic glances. Still, she thought she could keep this secret. It wasn't meant to be.

An old woman from across the aisle came up to Stevie. She was a vendor of herbs and potions and religious artifacts, and she had a knack for getting under his skin. She said to him, "Stevie, your wife's been gone for hours."

"And?"

"Do you care where she is?"

"No."

"Are you sure?"

"What do you want, old woman?"

"We took in a street kid. Do you remember him? The one that helped us load and unload."

"He stopped coming."

"Oh, he stopped helping us, but he didn't stop coming. He sells junk by the snack bar. We fired him because he stole merchandise from us."

"And?"

"Your wife's been talking to him every week, and today she's been down there all morning. What do you think of that?"

"What am I supposed to think?"

"*Ya casi se ven los cuernos.*"

"Speak English!"

"A man should know where his wife is and who she's making love to."

"María de la Luz," shouted the old woman's husband from across the way. "Come here."

"What row?" Stevie asked the old woman.

"Twenty-eight, left side, next to the watch repairman."

Stevie woke his son. "Penguin, come with me!"

"Yes, Papi," said the boy. He was cute. Really cute. The swap meet vendors nicknamed him Penguin because of the way he walked in his boots.

There were five hundred vendors in the swap meet. Almost all Mexican, except for some Korean, Chinese, and Salvadoran vendors, and there was an elderly Jewish couple who sold rayon material and an Arab woman who sold dresses, and in that maze of people and merchandise, Stevie set out with his boy and shovel to find his wife.

And, in aisle twenty-eight, they both saw Esmeralda sitting next to her lover. He was much younger than she, maybe even ten years, and he looked very macho in his tight black clothes and cowboy boots.

The man's tables were covered with blue gin bottles and wine glasses, old *Life* magazines, and a case full of coins. From a distance, Esmeralda seemed comfortable, as if she belonged there.

"Where you been?" Stevie asked Esmeralda.

"Shopping," she responded as she stepped away from her lover.

"Well, let's go," Stevie said.

"I'm not going with you anywhere!" she yelled.

"I'll break all this shit with my shovel!" shouted Stevie. "I mean it."

"What's the problem, amigo?" the young man said.

"Fuck you! I'm not your fucking amigo!" Stevie yelled.

"Fuck you, too! You fucking drunk!" the young man said as he raised his fists.

"Stop! Stop! I'll go," Esmeralda said as she pushed the young man's arms down and stood between the two.

"Penguin, come with me," she ordered.

Before she left, Esmeralda whispered something to her lover in Spanish. Then she walked several steps ahead of Stevie, dragging Penguin with her. Stevie walked with the shovel clenched in his hand. He didn't speak Spanish. Esmeralda spoke it anyway to annoy him. And it did annoy him. In fact, it tortured him. It reminded him just how incomprehensible she was. He realized how much he hated his life, and her, and the fucking swap meet. He felt like his insides were on fire.

When they got back to the stand, Esmeralda realized that Penguin had peed in his pants. The boy was so upset that he pushed her away and sobbed angrily by the truck.

Esmeralda said softly to him, "I'll buy you some new ones, okay?"

"No!" Penguin yelled. "Go away," he said as he pushed her hand away from him.

"Let's go to the restroom and get you changed," Esmeralda said as she struggled to get the boy to hold her hand.

"I want you back here in fifteen minutes or I swear I'll kick your ass and the ass of that stud of yours!" Stevie yelled at Esmeralda.

Esmeralda looked to see if the vendors had heard. Of course, they had. In fact, they were totally tuned into what was going on. She looked down and focused on her boy's hand.

"Buy me some lunch and get something for Penguin, and while you're at it, why don't you explain to Penguin what the fuck you were doing over there," Stevie blurted out. His speech was a little slurred. Penguin swooshed in his boots as he walked away with his mother.

Stevie reached for the ice chest and got a beer. It was his eighth beer. The last one in the ice chest. Stevie took a long swig and raised his beer can at the old woman across the aisle from him, but she looked away in disgust. Then, he raised it at Lucy, a raspy-voiced woman who sold cosmetics two spaces down. Lucy reached under the table and raised a can wrapped daintily with a pink napkin, and they both smiled.

It was noon and Stevie made three sales. A tape measure, a wrench, two screwdrivers. Then no sales. He turned in his chair and stared at Lucy's huge tits and the tattoos on her arm and chest. She had a red rose sprawling out from underneath her blouse. "Hey, Luuuucy," he shouted, but she ignored him. She had customers. He yelled again, "Oh, Luuuucy."

Lucy rolled her eyes at him and continued talking to her customers. Stevie stared at Lucy's dyed hair. It was long and wild and really shiny. She wore a tight, low-cut blouse. It was tie-dyed blue like the sky.

The swap meet speaker blared out, "Vendor, Stevie Escobar, please report to the snack bar immediately." The old lady vendor yelled out, "They're calling you."

Stevie got up and rushed clumsily to the snack bar. There, he found Penguin crying and an older, fat boy being held from the shoulder by the swap meet manager.

"He hit me and I hit him back," said Penguin, wiping his eyes and nose with his sleeve. "Then he pushed me and I fell and he kicked me in the face."

Penguin took a stuttering breath and then broke into a wail. "Look, Papi!" He held out a fist and opened it. Stevie saw two of his son's bloodied teeth.

"You stupid shit," Stevie yelled at the fat boy. "What if I kick your ass right now? You fucking bully."

Just then, Esmeralda rushed in, but as soon as she saw Stevie, she turned and walked out. Stevie followed her, grabbed her, and pulled her toward the video games where the tall black boxes created shadows, and there he slapped her hard. It ripped the skin on her lips.

Esmeralda pulled away from him, ran to Penguin, and then ran out of the snack bar. All the kids who saw what happened left the video games to tell their parents. And those who hadn't heard from their kids got to see the beautiful, bleeding woman running through the aisles of the swap meet with her weeping child.

She ran like women before her had run. Like La Malinche. Like La Llorona. Like a *puta*. Only those women had run on the beach, or along a river, or a canal. Or an alley.

Stevie sat by the Motorcade video game and stared at the steering wheel in front of him and then at the flashing scores on the screen. The simulated sound of racing cars blared. He got up and walked out of the snack bar.

He looked up, his hands above his eyes, and noticed the pigeons starting to hover over the swap meet. It was almost time to go home. As he walked back to his stand, he felt the stare of the vendors. "¡*Sinvergüenza*!" he heard a woman mutter in disgust.

All the vendors would know about the cheating and beating before the day was over. As far as Stevie was concerned, Esmeralda got what she deserved. He had a right to hit her. After all, she was *his* wife. It was the public display that was annoying to the vendors. It was a little too close to home. The vulgarities, the harshness, needed to be kept in-house. To display one's dirty laundry was, well, rude. Stevie thought they were all a bunch of hypocrites.

Esmeralda's lover was waiting for Stevie when he got back to his tent. Stevie could tell from the way Lucy was waving her hands that she was trying to get the crowd to disperse. When the young man saw Stevie, he ran to him and slammed his fist into Stevie's chest and socked him until his face was covered in blood. Stevie was too drunk to fight back. The young man yelled to Stevie, "Your wife's leaving you. I'm taking her to Mexico, to my family. I'm taking the boy."

"Fuck you!" was all Stevie could muster.

The man grabbed Stevie by the shirt and threw him hard. Lucy screamed. Someone yelled, "Call security." The lover jumped on Stevie again. It took three guys to pull him away.

When Stevie awoke, Lucy was splashing water gently on his face. She pressed a wet handkerchief against his temple. A security guard was asking him who hit him. The old woman vendor yelled out, "A thief. A thief hit him."

The security guard turned to her and said, "What did he take?"

The old woman replied, "His wife!"

Stevie heard her chuckle. He yelled, "You fucking old witch! Go to hell."

The swap meet emptied quickly. Lucy packed her lipsticks and nail polish in a suitcase. She knew Stevie was looking right at her, hoping she might have a kind word for him, a joke maybe, some flirtatious comment to lighten the mood, but she refused to make eye contact. She closed the suitcase, folded her small display table, placed both of them in the car trunk, and then carefully took down her umbrella.

Then, Stevie heard the sound of Penguin's boots, turned and saw the boy running toward him. Esmeralda was a few feet behind Penguin, chasing him, but she stopped as soon as she neared the tent. Penguin crashed into Stevie. "I'm not going to Mexico. I'm staying here with you."

"What did your mother tell you?"

"We're going to Mexico."

"And?"

"And I don't want to go to Mexico!"

"Go with your mother."

"NO."

Stevie grabbed him by the shirt collar. "Get out!"

Penguin took steps back.

"GET OUT!" yelled Stevie as he stood up.

Penguin ran away from Stevie and into his mother who pulled his ear hard as she walked away with him. Penguin kept looking back to see if Stevie was still looking at him. Stevie impulsively took a step forward, but he caught himself and awkwardly raised his hand as if he was saying good-bye.

It was three-thirty, and Lucy finished loading her merchandise and drove off without saying a word to Stevie. Stevie sat frozen in his lawn chair. He still hadn't packed a thing. Through the corner of his eyes, he could see an old man collecting empty cans and bottles. The old man crept quietly around Stevie, picking up all the beer bottles around the truck, even under it.

Vans and trucks full of tired faces plodded past Stevie. Most looked away, but a few looked right at him. Stevie thought he saw something in their faces, like fear or pain. He didn't know which. But then, what did it matter? They felt the same.

He stared at the pigeons swooping down for crumbs and at the empty drive-in screen in front of him. It was getting late. He wondered what movie they'd be showing tonight. Maybe a comedy or an adventure film. Perhaps a double billing. He thought, tonight, especially tonight, would be a good night for a comedy.

Ojitos

The way I see it, all the shit we're going through is on account of a cockroach. If my sister Marisela hadn't seen a cockroach on the motel bed, she wouldn't have refused to have sex with her boyfriend Carlos. And if she hadn't refused to have sex with Carlos, he wouldn't have gone to the motel owner and demanded his money back. And if Carlos wouldn't have been a fucking penny-pincher, arguing in front of everyone at the motel entrance, then Papi wouldn't have ever caught them red-handed.

But Papi did catch Carlos with Marisela at the motel, and everything went to shit because of it.

You see, Marisela had lied to Papi about going out with Carlos. She had told him that she was going to see a movie with a girlfriend. Although my sister is twenty-two, Papi prohibits boyfriends. If he knew about Carlos, he would get all the more infuriated because Carlos happens to work with us during the week at one of three sweatshops my father owns in Huntington Park. According to Papi, Carlos, who was recently hired as a quilter at one of the shops, is a peon, not at all the kind of man worthy of his daughter or of the huge financial possibilities of his business.

My family makes bedspreads. All kinds of bedspreads in all kinds of materials. Cotton bedspreads with ruffles, cotton bedspreads without ruffles, satin bedspreads, velvet bedspreads, bedspreads with ruffled pillow shams, floral bedspreads, lace bedspreads. My sister, Marisela, is an exceptionally skilled and hardworking seamstress. Without making a mistake, she can sew a ruffle onto a bedspread in twelve minutes flat. Papi has timed her. She also does all the accounts payable, the payroll, the quarterly taxes, and takes care of the business licenses and necessary insurances to keep the shops running. She rarely makes mistakes, and Papi claims she has a gift for remembering numbers. She is the brain of the family.

Every day after school, me and Marisela help Mami and Papi and the other workers finish their daily goal of $125 bedspreads per shop. On Friday, the week's inventory is counted and checked and shipped out or delivered to retailers. Profits are counted, and if everything is cleaned up by four, we have the rest of the afternoon off.

Marisela has been sleeping with Carlos for over seven months. He is the first man she has ever been with, and he has a hold on her that she isn't sure is love. But she has secretly promised to love him and to one day marry him anyway.

Papi has a hold on her too, and while she is sure that it is love, in fact a tremendous love she feels for her father, she isn't sure it's good for her. Papi's insistence that she not date, that she not prioritize school, that she invest all of her ambition into the business is a lot to ask, too much. (But she feels guilty about feeling this way. I would, too.)

Because of these two men and the holds they have on her, Marisela is reduced to lying to both of them. Aside from sewing a ruffle onto a bedspread in twelve minutes flat, she told me she feels lying is something she's gotten really good at. I've been pretty good at it myself considering I cover for her so much.

My family calls me "Ojitos"—little eyes because I squint a lot. Everyone seems to think I can handle the family history. I'm not so sure. The truth weighs on me. But, I am the intuitive one. The one who knows the secrets, the one who is all too aware of the liabilities of these secrets coming to light. I am the eyes of my family.

On this Friday evening, I felt nervous, really nervous, though I didn't know why. All day I noticed how irritable and fidgety Papi was. He shouted at me for not loading the merchandise into the truck fast enough, even though he usually doesn't let me load it alone, and then instead of taking the family out to dinner, he decided to stay at the shop and drink tequila with Eufemio, an older worker (and a drunk) who inspects and packages the bedspreads once the sets are complete.

It was ten at night on Friday when Papi drove up the driveway—four hours late. He didn't turn off the engine. He just sat in his Suburban and then lowered the window.

"Get in, you little liar," Papi yelled at me.

I saw how distracted he looked, how he tapped nervously on the steering wheel. I had been waiting for him on the porch, hoping he would take me to get a late-night pizza.

"Where's your sister?" Papi demanded.

"At the movies," I whispered.

"Where?" he yelled.

"At the movies," I insisted.

"You fucking little liar. You know damn well where your sister is."

I did, in fact, know that Marisela and Carlos were at that sleazy motel on Atlantic Boulevard. Marisela had confessed the whole affair to me the night she had lost her virginity. That night, Marisela had sneaked into bed with me. When she put her arms around me, I woke up. She pulled back my hair and whispered the details of the encounter: the nervousness, the struggle, the quickness, the pain, the bleeding. "Do I smell different?" she had asked me. From that first night, I had felt wrong about it, from that first night I felt dread in my gut.

As I climbed into Papi's Suburban, I asked, "Should I tell Mami?"

"Get the fuck inside now!"

When we got to the hotel corner, Papi stopped. I sensed danger, and I, out of nervousness, grabbed my knee. My knee was right next to the door handle.

Several minutes passed before we saw Marisela and Carlos arguing with the motel owner and then walking to Carlos's lowered Volkswagen Bug. Papi waited until they got into the car. Then he shifted violently in reverse and made a screeching turn into the parking lot, blocking Carlos's Bug, and jumped out of the car.

I heard Papi yelling into the car. "You shameless son of a bitch. Not with my daughter." He pulled Carlos out of the car, dragged him to a grassy area in front of the hotel lobby, and socked him in the face.

Carlos struggled to get up and swung awkwardly at Papi, who was twice as strong as him. He missed and fell into Papi who held him up, but up only so he could punch him again. "You shameless son of a bitch," Papi yelled. His voice broke. "Not with my precious daughter!" Carlos grabbed his nose and moaned. He remained face down on his knees.

Marisela jumped on Carlos, hugged him with her arms and legs. Papi yelled, "Get off of him, goddamnit," but she wouldn't budge. Papi had always been strict, but he'd never been mean. That day he was the meanest, most violent man in the world. Marisela later told me she thought he was going to kill Carlos.

When the Vietnamese owner heard Marisela's screams, he ran out to help Carlos. The man spoke softly to Papi in Spanish. "Let it go. He won't do it again. He's just a boy. He's learned his lesson."

I saw everything from a distance. Intuitively, I had walked next to the pay phone in front of the hotel while I witnessed the whole thing. I felt my heart pounding as I contemplated picking up the black receiver and calling 911. Only if he starts beating Marisela, I thought to myself.

A tall, shirtless man came running out of his hotel room, went to his semi, which was parked right next to the lobby, and pulled out a large, long, black flashlight. He held it like a weapon, extending it out and into Papi's chest. When Papi didn't react, the man got on his knees and looked at Carlos.

"Fuck!" Carlos moaned as if he was in a tremendous amount of pain. The layers of fat around the man's stomach wiggled as he tried to lift Carlos up from the ground. With his black Santana T-shirt, Carlos wiped his face. The shirt hid the lines of blood coming from his nose and mouth.

When Carlos straightened up, he looked right at Papi as he walked away as if to tell him he was just as much a man. With the help of the truck driver, he staggered toward his Volkswagen. When Marisela tried to follow him, Papi grabbed her by the arm and shouted, "Where the hell do you think you're going?"

Two years ago at a backyard party, I sat with my godfather and Papi as both men struggled to sober up. Papi was about as tired as he was drunk. Everyone wanted to go home, so Papi got up to wash his face.

My godfather called me to him. He was drunk, frighteningly drunk, and I sat tense next to him.

As he wrapped his arms around me, he said, "I'm very proud of your father, of his beautiful daughters, of his success with his business. You know I love him like a brother. I know he loves me like family, too. He's so hardworking, but he shouldn't be so difficult. He's too difficult. Just like his mother."

"You knew my grandmother?" I asked.

"Knew her? ¡*Chingado*! She's still alive and kicking!"

"But Papi told us she died."

"Well?" he said.

My godfather wasn't as smart as Papi, and he wasn't as shrewd a businessman. And he had two really fucked-up sons who were only in their teens and already serving time in Soledad. Envy is a powerful emotion, and my godfather was choking with envy at my father's success. So I knew my godfather wasn't beyond talking shit about Papi behind his back, even to his children. So I didn't take him too seriously.

"Where is she then?" I asked.

"In Tijuana. Where else? That's where your father was born."

"Papi's from Jalisco."

"No, he isn't. He's from Tijuana," he said.

"What about all that land grandmother inherited in Guadalajara?"

"Your grandmother was and is a *cantinera* in TIJUANA! They call her Dos Veces. Do you want to know why?"

I squinted my eyes and said nothing. Even if I didn't know my grandmother, I didn't like to hear someone talking shit about her.

"Because she lets you make love to her two times—one time for the drink and another for the cigarette," he laughed.

"And my grandfather?" I asked.

"*Eso sí, ¿quién sabe*? I bet your grandmother doesn't even know the answer to that one, but don't ever tell your father I told you. One of these days, someone's going to have to put that son of a bitch in his place. I have a right mind to . . . only I love him too much."

My godfather was referring to Papi being a major show-off. From the thick gold chain around his wrist, to his alligator boots, to his black Suburban, Papi was a cool cat, a smooth operator, a charmer, an embellisher of his accomplishments. And handsome. On hot days at the shop, Papi would work shirtless and challenge any of the workers to beat his speed at finishing the orders. No one could ever beat him. When it was all over, his biceps would shine with sweat. He's the muscle of the family.

At home, Papi often told crazy stories of how we were the descendants of rich Spanish landowners. *Gachupines,* he called them. He spoke passionately about the *gachupines*. When he told his stories, he moved his hands dramatically in circles, in scoops, as if every detail was a precious piece of family history.

Papi claimed he inherited his green eyes from his famous Spanish hacienda-owning father. His bright, piercing, roving eyes. But in all his stories, he never bothered to explain his dark bronze skin or his curly black hair.

Mami didn't know where her husband was that Friday night, nor did she care, since she was so busy finishing her orders. It was not uncommon that on a Friday evening he'd go out to eat or drink with a new client or with the workers. Anyway, Papi was happier being around people.

She, on the other hand, was quiet and soft-spoken. The middle child of eleven sisters, Mami had grown up in a small farming town in Michoacan. Farm life was hard, her family was very poor, and she had learned from an early age to work like a horse. "What God didn't give you in looks, he gave you in willingness," my mother had told me when I was young. So Mami was proud to have married a man like

Papi. Her drive and constancy were an attempt to measure up to him. Mami was total dedication to her husband, to her daughters, to her clients, and to her business. She was the resourceful one, the persistent one, the follow-through. Mami's the heart of the family.

On Friday night, she was busy at her overlock sewing machine in the garage, finishing a special order that needed to be delivered Saturday morning at a bridal shop in the garment district. A large part of the business was being reliable with the special orders. There was a wedding on Saturday evening, and the bride's family had ordered a special ruffled white satin bedspread for the nuptial bed. Mami was busy in the garage trying to finish all the extra lacework on the ruffles and on the cushions. From a tin box full of pieces of white lace from previous orders, Mami hand-sewed each piece of lace onto a cushion. She never threw anything away.

After her work in the garage, she planned to go to the kitchen and clean and soak the beans. Then, she would clean the cactus and take the meat out of the freezer and leave it to thaw overnight. Papi complained that she should show us how to cook so that all the work wouldn't fall on her, but she didn't want us to know how to cook, at least not to waste our lives away in a kitchen. Her girls were destined for better things than that.

When Papi came into the garage, we ran in after him. He stood before Mami, who was still sitting at her sewing machine, and told her that what had just happened was all her fault, that she had raised a bunch of whores for daughters, and that he was never going to forgive her for shaming him this way.

Mami rose from her chair, wrapped her arms around his waist, and tried pushing him onto the sewing machine chair so he'd calm down, but that only pissed him off more. He told Mami to get the hell away from him: " You're a whore like all the rest."

Those words went deep, and Mami's eyes were big and full of rage. She yelled back, "Don't blame us! You're the one that acts like an idiot! You're the one that can't control himself! You're the one . . ."

Papi threw her on the sewing machine and started choking her. He repeated over and over, "Shut up. Shut up. Shut your mouth."

He had her in a tight grasp and might have choked her to death if Marisela hadn't gotten the glass button jar from the shelf and smashed it on Papi's head, causing an explosion of glass and big yellow buttons. Papi grabbed the back of his head and, when he saw his hand was full of blood, he jerked back. He struggled to stand, then fell hard into the chair.

Mami yelled, "¡Ay, Ernesto!" as though she felt sorry for him and the next minute said, "It serves you right for being such a *pinche* bully." When they saw that he was out cold, the three picked him up and carried him off to bed.

When Papi woke up early the next morning, Mami was sitting on the porch drinking a cup of coffee. She hadn't slept at all. Without saying a word, Papi grabbed her by the arm and pushed her into the bedroom. I placed my ear on the door and heard a moan. And then another. For a second, I thought maybe they were making love. But then Papi threw open the door and walked out. Mami was muffling her sobs with the pillow.

"She's mine!" Papi yelled.

"She's not yours. She's our daughter, but she's not yours," Mami replied.

"But everything I've done has been for all of you. I've done my part. Is it too much to ask you to be *decente*?"

"They have to leave home. Whether you like it or not. And what nonsense is it to try to control anyone when they're in love?"

"You call this love?"

"They've done their part. They help you as much as they can."

"That shameless son of a bitch will get her pregnant and then leave her. And then who'll pick up the bill? I'm not working my ass off for that asshole. She leaves him or I leave. Which is it?"

All the attention turned toward Marisela. Marisela was so shocked she couldn't cry. She clung to Papi's arm and said, "Don't go, I'll go. He'll marry me. He said he'd marry me." But Papi shrugged her off. "Are you going to stop seeing him or not?"

There was a long pause, and tears started running down Marisela's face. "I love him," she said.

Papi went to the kitchen and got a trash bag and then went to his closet, opened his hands wide, and with one swoop got all his hanging shirts and shoved them in a bag.

I had the car keys in my overall pocket. I also had the shop keys in case they needed a place to spend the night. I thought of keeping them and letting Papi calm down. But not finding the keys just made Papi more violent, so I slammed the keys on the kitchen table in front of him. He looked shocked at me, and then took the keys and left.

When Papi left, the three shops closed down, but I guess for both Mami and Papi, being businesspeople was at the core of their being, so even if their hearts were broken, they both went back to work two weeks later, Mami at one shop and Papi at the other.

They used our godfather to communicate between them. Six months later, the third shop was sold to my godfather who promised to pay them fifty-fifty as soon as he got the cash.

A year later, Mami and Papi became intense competitors. Mami had the advantage because she had us on her side, but Papi had the rage and that was enough to last a lifetime.

He harassed his customers not to buy from us. He would interrogate customers, remind them that a business deal was about trust, and if there wasn't trust, there wasn't a deal. When Don Eugenio came into his shop and confessed that he bought half of his merchandise with Papi and the other half with Mami claiming, "It's only fair," Papi showed him out of the shop, slammed the door in his face, and shouted through the door, "Buy it all from them, you fucking backstabber."

Mami wasn't like that at all. She knew some of the customers would buy from both her and Papi, and she wouldn't say anything about it. Occasionally, she'd let one of the workers walk over to his shop to take him food. The workers said that he had lost a tremendous amount of weight and that he drank too much.

But Papi was determined to steal all of Mami's customers and would have done it too, had he not surrendered to booze. The seamstresses said that he slept at the shop, that his bed was a pile of rags, and that he was always dirty, unshaven, and drunk.

Eventually, we heard rumors about Papi hooking up with another alcoholic, some prostitute from Honduras. We heard different versions of how Papi and his new girlfriend would get drunk together and have fistfights in front of the workers. When Mami heard about Papi's lover, she went into a depression. She was quieter than ever.

I went to ask my godfather to please help Papi, so he tried to take Papi to an AA meeting. According to my godfather, Papi got into the car with him, showered him with love, declared his lifelong loyalty, and then got out. As he slammed the door, Papi told my godfather to never look for him again.

A month later, the workers showed up at the shop and saw a piece of paper taped to the door saying that Papi had sold the equipment and closed the shop for good. And then Papi disappeared. That was a shock to us because even though he had left home, he was in the neighborhood. Now he was gone, really gone, like he was dead or something.

Another year passed, and no one had heard from Papi. Marisela married Carlos, and they moved in with Mom and me. Carlos tried hard to be responsible. He dropped out of school and got a job at the gas station. Once his schedule became regular, Marisela convinced him to go back to night school.

In my American Literature class, I got to discuss the immigrant experience in the United States. My class read *Snow Falling on Cedars*, *Rain of Gold*, and *Jasmine*. For two months, I wrote about different aspects of my own immigrant experience in a journal. For the final, the teacher gave us a creative writing assignment; we had to write a real or fictive immigrant memoir.

I thought of writing a story based on my own experiences. It would be a story of how my immigrant family collapsed, of how the whole thing fell apart. I wrote that although Mexican immigrants don't have a lot, they do have family. That's what we hold on to, to make life livable, to survive the tough times. And yet the immigrant family is hardly resilient or malleable. It can, as in my case, be fragile and brittle. It can break or snap or explode into nothing. And why? Because a woman had sex. And not only did she have sex, but she had sex with someone she wanted to, with someone she wasn't married to, someone that the family had not accepted. A woman, I concluded, can either lie to her family or to herself. I'm not sure which is worse.

I am sure that daughters of immigrants should take refuge within themselves. They must guard their passion. Keep the fire deep within them, because their world is not ready for it. These secrets should remain caved within their hearts so that the fire will not die out completely. That way the next generation of daughters will have a flicker to clasp onto.

The Catholic Girl

"Mary Magdalene," Susana said.

"Nonsense! If you can't take the sacrament of confirmation seriously, we won't confirm you at all," Ms. O'Hara said. "Go see Brother David in the chapel after school today. If you haven't resolved this issue by then, you will not, young lady, get confirmed."

Ms. O'Hara had been a nun for a long time, in fact until Vatican II, when she and everyone else in her order left in protest. But everything about Ms. O'Hara, from her pudgy, white cheeks, to her short, white hair, to her rigid, cold ways was very nunlike. She called herself a feminist, but deep down she wanted to take a cattle prod to many of these girls. Today, she especially wanted to hit Susana for being so unruly. "How could any child want to name herself after a prostitute?" she sighed.

Susana walked to her school's chapel and knelt at the altar, made the sign of the cross, and sighed, "Mary, Mary, Mary." In the darkness she watched the candle flames flicker. Fifteen minutes passed and no Brother David.

The altar was full of white roses, and on the Virgin's foot hung a blue ribbon with the inscription *Forever in our hearts*

Jason. The office secretary's baby had been stillborn. Susana had heard about it in the lunchroom.

"You know, Jason, they can't cut you a deal if you're stillborn. Rules state it's purgatory for you," she thought to herself. "If it was up to me, I'd send you straight to heaven. And of course, Mary Magdalene would cut you a deal 'cause she knows about compromising circumstances. Mary Mother might too, but Mary Virgin, forget it. You're out."

Then she heard Brother David's soft whistle, "Hail Holy Queen," and the gentle thud of his sandals as he moved toward her. Susana's palms were sweaty, and she started slapping them gently on her lap, and without realizing it she started whistling too, "for it's one, two, three strikes you're out at the old ball game."

Brother David wore garb that hung heavy and full with a rope knotted around his waist. He was middle-aged and not a handsome man, in fact, rather unattractive, with a W.C. Field's nose, a serious bald spot, and about a hundred excess pounds, but he was the only man on that campus, except for the gardener. And he enjoyed this fact. He considered himself counselor, confessor, teacher, and, not least of all, mentor to all these teenaged girls on the hill.

Brother David and Susana sat sideways on the pew. His one leg extended. "Well," he said. "I hear you're having trouble finding a name for yourself, so I took the liberty and brought my favorite book of saint names to see if together we might come up with something." He took a small red book from under his garb and started reciting slowly, "Saint Anne, patron saint of housewives, Saint Barbara, patron saint of architects, Saint Margaret Clitherow, patron saint of businesswomen, Saint Joan of Arc, patron saint of soldiers, now that's a popular one around here," he said and went on, his head inside the red covers of the book.

"I want Mary Magdalene," she said quietly.

"Well, that's impossible," he said abruptly. "Don't you understand that you pick a saint name because you want that saint to be a kind of role model, someone to look up to. How can you look up to a prostitute? For goodness sakes!"

"Dr. Smith said that her story was about redemption. And maybe she didn't have a choice. Maybe she was a prostitute because she had to. And how would you know anything about prostitution anyway?" Susana yelled the last part. An awkward silence followed, and Susana realized that this was strike one.

"Well, I can't seem to remember when a young lady has been more disrespectful. I find it amazing that you survived your junior year with that attitude. I don't remember you being as shameless before. What you need to do is confess yourself."

Brother David took out a long piece of white cloth that he kissed and placed around his neck. He closed his eyes for a minute, muttered some lines, and then gave Susana a "come on" look.

"Bless me, father, for I have sinned . . ." Susana took a deep breath. "These are my sins." She paused. "How can you expect me to remember them all just like that?"

"Go through the commandments," he snapped. "Have you ever . . ."

"No," Susana said abruptly.

"Have you ever . . ."

"No," she said.

"Do you attend Mass every Sunday?"

"No," she said.

"You do not attend Mass every Sunday?"

"No," she said.

"And why not?"

"My parents work on Sunday."

"And they love money so much that they work on the Sabbath? What kind of parents are they?"

"They work because they have to," Susana said angrily.

"What do they do?"

Susana paused. No one at school knew. Not even her closest friends. She had lied about it until now, and she knew that this was truly her most grievous sin. "They clean hotel rooms."

"A scholarship student. It's obvious to me, young lady, that you do not appreciate your education."

Susana started slapping her palms on her lap again. A "fuck you" was knotted in her throat. She instinctively held her chin up hoping it would slide back down.

"What I think we need to do is call your parents and set up a conference, to see if maybe we can do something about your attitude."

"They barely speak English," said Susana, mincing her words.

"Well, I guess we'll have to get a translator. I don't think we can rely on you to translate. Can we?" He took out a little notebook and a pen from the layers of brown cloth on him and started writing something in it.

She hated him. Hated him with a passion, but as long as he had that white cloth around his neck, she knew she couldn't tell him what an asshole he was. She yelled, "For these . . . and all my sins I am truly SORRY!"

"I have not given you your penance!" he yelled. "And you are not sorry! Get out! I am not absolving you. Tomorrow bring your parents. Meet me after school in the dean's office."

Strike two.

It was usually a ten-minute bus ride home, but today she felt like walking, even if it was ninety degrees out. She needed time to organize her thoughts before she got home. There was no sense in translating the day's events. She needed to *think* in Spanish, reinterpret and package everything, so her mother wouldn't get hysterical.

As Susana exited the school gates, a steady flow of minivans, Mercedes, and BMW's filled the campus parking lot.

When she was a ninth grader, Susana's father would pick her up every day in his old Chevy truck full of mops, brooms, buckets, and gallons of cleansers all tossing about in the back. Susana was hyperconscious of the fact that all her classmates were looking out their windows to see who was in the truck.

Every day for her ninth and tenth grade year, she refused to mix with the other girls after school while she waited for her father to pick her up. The moment he would drive in, she'd get in, slam the door closed, smack the lock down with her elbow, swing the shoulder strap across her, and buckle herself in, consumed presumably in what she was doing and oblivious to the rest of the world. Then, she bought some black Ray Bans, which she never took off, rain or shine, as long as she was outdoors. These precious visors helped her in her quest for anonymity.

It was May and the sun shone strong. She felt the itch of her nylon-wool socks, the heat burning through the soles of her penny loafers. Her bra was completely perspired. She walked into the driveway, sweaty and tired, and saw him in the backyard watering his camellias. Her father wore his sombrero, and his pants were rolled up. Water trickled out of the hose he held in his hand. It was easy imagining him in some field in Mexico, thirty years before.

Her father didn't have the Catholic fervency that her mother did. He was Mexican, so he was Catholic. It was a kind of package, and he had no problems with it. Though he didn't promote it either, and Susana appreciated that since she always felt restless around the topic of religion.

"Have you eaten?" he said in his thick accent.

"No."

"Go eat, then come help me with the camellias."

"I don't want to go to school anymore."

"Any school?"

"I don't want to go to this school."

"Why?"

"I'm not comfortable anymore."

"Do they treat you bad?"

"No. I'm just not comfortable anymore."

"Where will you go?"

"Public school."

"You only have a year left."

"I know."

There was a long silence. She remembered her parents' excitement when they found out that Susana could attend Catholic school. How they had to scrounge enough money to pay for books, uniforms, and all those required retreats. Susana had long thought about how hard they worked, and it made her feel guilty, really guilty. Her parents worked ten-hour shifts. Six days a week, sometimes seven. And all for this. For this suburban house, for this small camellia garden, so that Susana could go to Catholic school and be raised around white people. And she, blessed daughter of Raúl and Elnora García, hated it.

"It's okay," he said. "Everything will be okay," he said with such sadness that Susana's heart literally ached. Susana grabbed the dying camellias and tore them carefully from their buds, then went out to the alley and emptied her bucket of dead camellias into the trash bin while her father pruned the bushes.

An excruciating long silence followed until her father spoke. "Do you want me to go with you tomorrow?"

Susana knew what that meant. Her father wouldn't put up a fight. He never did. He would nod, "Yes, Brother David," "Of course, Brother David," "You've been so kind and patient and understanding, Brother David." He'd plead for Susana, put his hand over his chest the way he almost always did when he spoke to figures of authority. As if he was taking off his sombrero and placing it over his chest. It was ingrained in him to cow down to authority. Susana fucking hated it.

"No," Susana replied, "But please tell Mami."

Susana sneaked out early the next morning to avoid the commotion her mother would make when she found out, but in her chemistry lab Susana had images of her mother cupping her face, crying, yelling out that this was a terrible omen, or slamming a pan on the stove while she blamed it all on her father.

It was three-thirty when she walked slowly to the dean's office. The office was beyond the parking lot, and the path was full of blooming jacarandas. A breeze whisked the lilac flowers past her as she walked by.

Susana's palms grew sweaty as she neared his office. She began to whistle, "Take me out to the ball game, take me out with the crowd, buy me some peanuts . . . " She could see Brother David through the window chatting with Ms. Dennis, the Spanish teacher. He opened the door and immediately shouted, "Where is your father? You will not be accepted in school if you do not bring your father or mother!"

"I spoke to my father yesterday, and he wasn't able to come today."

Ms. Dennis hurried out of the room.

"Young lady, you're trying every ounce of patience I have. Sit down!" He picked up the phone. "Ms. O'Hara, can you please call Susana García's parents at once and tell them to pick her up." He pulled his chair from behind his desk and placed it directly in front of Susana.

"They're not home," Susana said as she sank into the sofa.

"Well, then, maybe we won't release you until they come home."

He lowered the hydraulic chair and sat there with his legs crossed. His left foot nearly swung in front of Susana's chest.

"I think we should begin with a prayer, so we can bridge into a discussion of your poor attitude. O heavenly Father . . ."

Susana stared at the red saint book still on Brother David's desk. She remembered the drawing of Mary Magdalene looking up at the blue sky, her eyes lazily half closed, and her mouth slightly open in a moment of spiritual ecstasy.

Something deep within her propelled Susana to open her mouth too. She looked up at the ceiling, but there wasn't much happening up there, so she focused on the rope around Brother David's waist. It was a thick rope. A stupid, pretentious rope that symbolized humility or something like that. A heavy rope that pulled her down, down to his exposed toe. A toe that was fat and long and hairy.

Susana looked away at the pine-green carpet and then right at Brother David's toe. And then away again. Her mouth still ajar, she half-closed her eyes and thought of spiritual ecstasy.

"And forgive us our trespasses," Brother David muttered with an intensity and movement that helped Susana lose herself in the moment.

Susana felt heat flare up within her, the intensity of her anger becoming desire. It was an energy that was both powerful and alluring. She leaned toward the toe, her mouth slightly open, her lips extended.

When Susana opened her eyes, she saw utter horror and shock on Brother David's face. He was looking right at her. His toe was hanging out in the middle of nowhere, like the plank off a ship. She puckered her lips in an exaggerated way.

"Well, I never!" he stammered and stood up.

Flustered and out of words, he walked to the window, away from her, and as he ran his hand through his hair, he yelled, "Say the Hail Mary with me now! On your knees," he demanded.

Susana sat where she was. Her palms slapped her thighs. She rocked back and forth. "Blessed art thou amongst women," Susana moaned fervently. Her gold cross swung between her breasts. "Blessed are the fruits . . . " she moaned as she cupped her breasts with both hands. For a long moment, their eyes met. Susana stared in the intense, dull blue eyes of Brother David. Hard, uncompromising eyes that glared at her, but as Susana bowed her head down, Brother David's eyes followed, and for another long moment he stared at that space between the second and third buttons of her blouse, that opening that widened when Susana pulled her shoulders back, when the largeness of her breasts became more apparent. And for a fallible second or two, Brother David looked at the nipple that leaned toward his toe.

"Stop!" he yelled.

"What?" Susana yelled.

Brother David walked out of the room, slammed the door behind him, and paced outside until Ms. O'Hara arrived. Susana could see them disagreeing with one another through the window blinds.

When they turned and saw Susana looking at them, they stepped away from the window. Susana heard Ms. O'Hara interrupting Brother David, "How can I justify this? She's an honor student. We've never had trouble with her before."

Then Brother David shouted, "That's final."

After a while, Ms. O'Hara walked in and said, "I'm afraid that Brother David is deeply offended by your attitude. He believes this is not the appropriate school for you. Though you were given the opportunity to succeed here, you haven't appreciated what was being offered to you. Your parents should have been here. In any case, they can confer with us if they choose, but Brother David is adamant about his decision . . . "

Strike three.

That afternoon, Susana walked home again. She took a short cut through the park and sat on a bench under a shady tree. She felt butterflies in her stomach at the thought of having to explain her dismissal to her parents. But at the same time, she felt a sense of relief. Next year, she'd be bussed across town to a public school where there would be other Mexican girls, and that would be fine. At least she wouldn't feel like such a misfit. And there would be working-class parents there too. And her mother would survive the rejection, Susana told herself, because she'd still go to college. And she'd go to a college someplace far, far away from this suburban hell.

She took off her penny loafers, rolled down her socks, put her head back, and had several peaceful thoughts about jacaranda flowers whisking past her, about camellias, even about some far-off farmland in Mexico she had never seen.

Pinky Sandoval

"A man shouldn't have more beautiful hair than his lover," Elvira said as she stroked his long, black hair. His hair was utterly beautiful to her but in an indeterminate way. She couldn't decide if it was too shiny, or too thick, or just too damn long. She reached over his chest and singled out one long strand, measuring it against his body. It almost reached his belly button.

"It's too long. Let me cut it," she said.

"Pinky" was nicknamed by his brothers because he was the fifth of five and kind of lanky. His real name was Rolando. And that's what Elvira called him. Rrrrolando. With her rolling rrs.

"I like my hair," he said softly. He stared at the attractive middle-aged woman next to him.

Elvira's hair was a dirty blonde, and it looked like it had been touched too much. Most of the women at her beauty salon had the same type of hair. Ten feet away, it looked like a work of art, but up close you could see how tired it was of being handled. There was nothing natural about it. When he first started dating Elvira, he noticed how her hair would look like a million bucks when he knocked on her door, and then how all those curls would collapse into nothing when they were in bed together.

But he liked her hair anyway. He liked everything about her. He'd rather be with her over any woman his own age.

"I want you to cut your hair. Cut it for me," she said.

He shook his head. No. No. No. He kissed her neck, moved his hands around her, and tried to cajole her into making love. Perhaps she would forget about his hair.

Pinky was nineteen, and his hair was very important to him. He thought it expressed who he was—the aspiring muralist. As the strands grew out of him, so his art budded, his sense of self emerged. And he wanted to tell her so, but she pulled back, away from him.

"Did you hear what I said?" she demanded.

"But I thought you liked it. I thought it made me look sexy."

She shook her head. "It makes you look too much younger than me. And I don't like that. I didn't like the way that woman stared at me at Denny's."

Elvira and Pinky had caused quite a commotion yesterday morning at Denny's when he took a piece of waffle from his plate and fed it to her. The waffle had whipped cream on it and a bit of strawberry, and Elvira did a wondrous thing with her tongue when she took it off his fork. A group of old women was sitting across from them. One of them said loud enough for everybody to hear that a young man shouldn't be with such an older woman, and that there was too much perversity in this world, and that Judgment Day was coming and everyone was going to hell. The restaurant was almost empty, and the whole thing didn't really bother Pinky. That is, not until now.

"Because of that fucking old woman and her fucking warped . . . " Pinky stopped. He felt the anger rising in him, but he didn't want to be angry. All he wanted was to please this woman. He grabbed her and kissed her hard, and when she resisted he kissed her harder, and then she succumbed.

But that same night Pinky had a difficult time sleeping. He thought maybe he had eaten too late or maybe had too many beers. Eating late always upset his sleep. He'd dream about dead relatives, or massacres, or being chased through a jungle. This morning, he couldn't even remember what he had dreamt. All he could feel was the sense of exhaustion of having to run miles and miles in his dreams. That's when his mother called.

Mom went straight to the point. She was going to die soon—from heartbreak—and it was all Pinky's fault.

"I worked so hard all my life, so that you could lead a decent one, and what do I get in return? Huh? Is this what you call love? Is this how you form a family? I want you to leave her. Leave her and go to church."

"Mom, please. You know I can't do that," Pinky whispered into the phone. Elvira stopped before closing the bathroom door and gave him a knowing smirk.

"*¡Sinvergüenza!*" his mother yelled. "But you *can* sleep with her. You *can* live in sin." She paused. "I called your father."

"What?"

"He's coming tonight. His flight arrives at nine at the Tijuana airport. I want you to go pick him up."

"Why is he coming?" Pinky's voice was starting to rise. "I can't pick him up."

"You have to. He's expecting you."

Pinky hung up the phone. He went back to bed and stared at the ceiling, and when Elvira came out of the bathroom he stared at her, at how the little towel wrapped so nicely around her head, at how the bigger towel wrapped tightly around her chest.

He watched her as she stared into her three vanity mirrors, the one right in front of her, and the two smaller ones to the left and right of her. It was true that Elvira was almost twice his age. And it was also true that he should have gone to college instead of staying in the neighborhood. But artists educate themselves, he thought.

Well, when Elvira saw how upset Pinky was, she rescheduled all her appointments, called Pinky's boss and told him Pinky was sick, and then snuck into bed with him again. Pinky felt bad, really bad. But it wasn't too long before Elvira made him forget all about his father. Two hours later, they were both exhausted, and they slept soundly until the afternoon.

When he woke up at four in the afternoon, a wave of panic overcame him. He pictured his father waiting for him at the airport with all the boxes of coffee and coconut candies no one ever ate. He saw his father in his Sunday clothes waiting for him. Pinky remembered how his father's breaths would get short and abrupt right before he was going to yell at him. Just then the phone rang.

Pinky jumped out of bed. "Don't answer it!"

"Let me take care of it, Rolando."

"No. Don't answer."

She got up anyway and picked up the phone. By the time she turned to look for Pinky, he already had his pants and shoes on and was headed for the door.

"Where are you going?" Elvira yelled at him.

"I'll be back," Pinky said.

Elvira placed her hand on the phone receiver. "You know that they're not going to stop unless you put your foot down."

"He's waiting for me."

"I don't want you to go," Elvira said. There was a small break in her voice.

"I gotta go," Pinky said as he closed the door. Elvira was too good-looking a woman to ask twice, and he knew it. But in that nanosecond between his hand and the doorknob, he sensed that whatever he did, she'd take him back. At least this one time.

Pinky's parents were not divorced. They weren't even separated. They just didn't live together. In fact, they lived happily not together.

His dad had been a factory worker in the garment district. When he fell and broke his hip, he had to go permanently on disability. That freaked him out. He went into a deep depression. He lost thirty pounds and walked around all day in his pajamas. He tried physical therapy, herbal medication, acupuncture, but nothing helped him out of it. Until he found pigeons.

One of the drunks, Bigotes, in the pool hall down the street from their house gave his father six pigeons. The idea was to eat them because apparently deep-fried pigeons are very tasty, and Bigotes longed for a decent home-cooked meal, but his dad felt bad about eating them, so he made a wire cage for them on the back patio. In no time, six became fifteen. And then fifteen became sixty.

Anyway, the week of the big fight between Oscar de la Hoya and Julio César Chávez, Pinky's dad got the notion to send a note out with one of the pigeons. The note read, *Who'll it be? Chávez or de la Hoya?*

Being Mexican, Pinky's father was obviously partial to Julio César Chávez, and he bet fifty bucks on the Mexican fighter. But then the note came in. And it said, *The Pocho will win.* The Pocho will win. Well, Pinky's dad didn't believe in the Pocho's power punch, but he thought that this wasn't just any ordinary note. This was a note delivered by some divine intervention, so he withdrew his fifty-dollar bid on Chávez and placed the mortgage check, five hundred dollars, on de la Hoya. When de la Hoya won, he was convinced that the pigeons were "special" messengers. It was four to one, so he made two thousand dollars, and he invested in more pigeons and started writing more notes.

But it all came to an end when Health Services was called in because of the smell of the pigeons, and more specifically the pigeon crap, which was causing the neighbors distress. Apparently, their shit is literally explosive. The old man next door said that he developed a hacking, dry cough because of it.

Pinky's dad was ordered to tear down his pigeon shed and get rid of his precious pigeons. The whole thing depressed him so much that he decided he was better off in Mexico, in his hometown where things like this didn't happen.

Pinky's mom agreed, and since they were getting older, it was better to start setting up a retirement home down south in case they needed to give up their home for one of their sons, since that was all they had to give them. For them, it was worth the two or three years that they had spent apart.

By the time Pinky got to the Tijuana airport, his father's jacket was folded over his arm, and his sleeves were rolled up.

Pinky jumped out of his car, gave his father a hug, and then proceeded to quickly shove his two suitcases and the boxes of coffee and coconut candy in the back seat.

As soon as he snapped in his seatbelt, Pinky's father asked about Pinky's oldest brother.

"He's all right."

"And your other brothers?"

"Fine."

"And your mother?"

"All right."

"Is that all you have to say?" Pinky's father yelled at him.

"What do you want me to say? They're fine."

"Do you even know? Your mother says you haven't been home in over two months. Is that true? She says you found a job painting walls."

"I'm not a painter. I'm a muralist."

"What the hell does that mean? Do they pay you?"

"They will after they get funded."

"So how are you getting by? Who the hell is supporting you?"

"I have a girlfriend."

"That's what I heard," he said. "What kind of man lets a woman support him? Better yet, what kind of woman allows for this?"

"My kind of woman, I guess."

"You guess wrong, *cabrón,*" Pinky's father shouted. His face was inches away from Pinky's. "Do you know why we had you? Do you? Because your mother and I wanted a family. A man's duty in life is to have a family. Do you hear me? To have children."

"It's not what I want."

"I don't care what you want. It doesn't matter what you want. I didn't say it was your desire to have a family. I said it was your duty. You're going to do what you need to do. Do you hear me?"

Pinky was silent, but he was steaming inside. He wanted to punch the steering wheel or break the window or slam on the brakes so that his head would go crashing into the windshield. He fucking hated it when his father did this to him.

"Stop in Oceanside, I'm hungry," his father said. "I want a filet o' fish."

Because it was way past midnight, McDonald's was closed, so they stopped at a 7-Eleven. There, Pinky's father got out and bought two hot dogs and a beer. Pinky's father ate beef, pork, and fish, but not chicken. He had stopped eating poultry when he became obsessed with pigeons.

Pinky placed his forehead down against the steering wheel and thought to himself that he wanted nothing more than to go home and go to sleep. But his father took his time taking swigs from his paper-bagged beer as he leaned against the car. After he finished his beer, he bit slowly into his hot dogs. Pinky stayed in the car, but out of respect and fear, he lowered the window so he could hear his father speak to him.

"I know that duty isn't everything," his father said slowly. "A man's a man. He's got needs. Desires. Ambitions. That's part of the difficulty in being a man."

Pinky didn't know what he meant, but he kind of liked it. It sounded reasonable.

"Did I ever tell you that male pigeons lactate?" his father said.

"They what?"

"They lactate. The males breast-feed their young. Did you know that?"

Pinky did a double take at his father's non sequitur. He was still trying to understand the part about having needs.

"I didn't know."

"Well, I didn't breast-feed you."

Pinky breathed a sigh of relief.

"But it hurts me well enough to hear what you're up to. You'll never be able to form a decent family with that woman. Understand what she is and what she isn't."

"What isn't she?"

"That's why when your mother called me, I bought a plane ticket for the first flight back. I flew back for you."

Pinky looked at his father's paunchy, middle-aged chest. His father's breasts, if he had to think of them as woman's *chichis*, as lactating *chichis*, would be rather small. The thought was more than disturbing.

"A man doesn't have to breast-feed his child to feel every misstep he makes," his father muttered to himself.

When they got home, his father said to him, "Come on Friday. Your mother is cooking something special for you. At four. Don't be late."

"But I work on Friday," Pinky replied quickly. It was a lie.

"You can get out of work early. Don't disappoint me or your mother," his father said. "Oh, and son, please, for the love of god, please cut off that damn hair."

Pinky took off his shoes before he got to the front door of Elvira's condo, tiptoed across the kitchen, and snuck into bed. He reached over to embrace Elvira's waist, thinking she was asleep, but she was totally awake.

"What did *daddy* have to say?" she snapped as she threw Pinky's hands off of her.

"I just went through hell and back, Elvira," Pinky said halfheartedly. "Give me a break."

"Next time, don't come back," Elvira snapped. "I'm tired of dealing with you when you act like a little boy."

"You like the little boy in me," Pinky smiled at her.

"Not always," she said.

"Come on, baby, let's be happy," Pinky said. "How can I make it up to you? Huh? What would make you happy?"

"Come on, then," she replied as she got out of bed and disappeared into the hallway. "Come on," she repeated.

Her panties, a satiny piece of lilac, were by the bed. Pinky grabbed them up off the carpet, tucked them under the pillow, and then followed her.

The bar stool stood alone in the middle of the kitchen.

"Sit," she said.

She took an old plastic shower curtain from the closet and wrapped it around Pinky. He could see Elvira by looking at a shiny skillet hanging from the wall. Elvira's hand pulled back forcefully as she combed his hair. He started to feel scared, really scared.

"You can cut up to the shoulder, that's it. Do you understand?"

"*Sí, mi amor,*" she said softly as she braided his hair, wrapping one clump of hair around the other until she got to the bottom. Pinky heard the snap of her rubber band.

She's the devil straight from hell, Pinky thought to himself. His father's words rang in his head.

Elvira pulled down hard on his hair and then with several swift snips, she cut it off. He felt his head fall forward.

"Let me straighten the rest," Elvira said as she casually swung his heavy, twelve-inch, limp braid onto his lap. Pinky instinctively grabbed his throat. His fingers could feel the rapid pulsing of his heart.

"You're not going to throw it away, are you?" Pinky said fearfully.

"Of course not," she said. "I'll put it away in one of my drawers."

Elvira went to sleep right after that, but Pinky stayed up drinking beers and watching reruns. He feared sleep. He'd have another nightmare, and he knew it. He decided that he would visit his parents on Friday. They'd be happy to see that his hair had been cut. And he'd agree to enroll in community college. It was for the best, after all. He'd tell his father that Elvira was a passing thing, a place to sow his wild oats. His father would like that. Everyone would be happy except him.

As he took a swig of his beer, Pinky made an oath to himself that one day he'd have a vision quest and turn public space into something beautiful, something meaningful for those who passed it. One day, he would dream the way a shaman dreams. He'd do this in spite of his world of duty and dependence. Deep down, he knew he wasn't supposed to be a plumber, or a baker, or a teacher, or a lawyer. He had been bestowed with a talent. And so be it. He would shut out the rest of the world as if he were blind and deaf and dumb. He would sit and wait and listen until his heart beckoned him again.

Somewhere Between Santa Monica and Incarnación de Cristo

Last December, Walter, my husband, started complaining that having my parents live with us was more than he could handle. I really didn't know what to say. Mexicans tend to live together, and I was comfortable having them there with me. I tried to cajole Walter into accepting the situation. "The house is cleaner, food is always in the fridge or on the stove, and you never have to do any of the yard work. What else do you want?"

But Walter said he was sick of Spanish soap operas, sick of beans with eggs, beans with meat, beans in soup, and that we could just as well hire the neighbor's gardener to do the yard work.

"They go, or I go," he said while I ate my cereal on Saturday morning.

"Well, then, I guess I'll see you later," I responded flatly.

I've never expressed anger or sadness well, not even at critical moments. Actually, even less at critical moments. (My two bleeding ulcers confirm that I do stress out quite often, though.) It wasn't like I was even trying to act hard. He had just caught me off guard.

"Fuck you!" He slammed the table so hard, the milk from my bowl spilled into my lap.

Two hours later, he was gone. He took the duffle bag full of socks and T-shirts and our Chihuahua, Frito.

I thought he'd be gone a day or two, but a week later, he still hadn't even called.

I was able to lie to my parents about Walter being gone for a couple of days. I thought I was protecting them by not telling them the truth, but they already knew what was going on and sat me down and told me they were leaving.

"Your father and I have decided to visit your cousins in Michoacán."

"You haven't seen them in twenty years," I responded.

"Well, it's about time. Don't you think? We better go while we still can."

"You don't have to go, you know," I said.

I would have said other things, but I felt a choking sensation in my throat, so I stopped. I figured they knew how much I loved them and wanted them with me. Words are so cheap nowadays, anyway.

A tremendous sense of loneliness overcame me when I went to the travel agency to pick up their plane tickets. There was no return flight. When I tried to change it, the travel agent told me it wasn't a mistake—my father hadn't requested a flight back home.

For a moment, I thought about going to Mexico with them. I hadn't been to their hometown since I was twelve. All I remember was how remote it was. We took a truck up a mountain for about five hours, and when the road stopped, we saddled up a horse. I remember crying all night because the horsehairs gave me an unbearable skin rash. There was no toilet, no shower, and we only had running water two hours in the morning and again for a short time at night. It was a horrible experience.

One week later, I saw them off at the airport. They had two huge suitcases and two carry-ons each, the maximum allowed. Each piece of luggage was filled with things for family they hadn't seen in over twenty years.

When the customs officer opened my mother's suitcase to inspect it, he couldn't close it again. He left it there for my father to try, but it just wouldn't shut.

"How did you close it at home?" I snapped.

"I sat on it," Mom replied. Then she looked at me. "You sit on it."

"I'm not sitting on it! Jesus Christ!" But when I saw the long line of people looking at us, I got on my knees and pressed as hard as I could against the case while my mother struggled with the zipper.

I yelled at her, "The last time you saw my cousins they were teenagers. They're in their thirties now. How the hell do you know these clothes will fit 'em?"

"All the men in the family are short and fat. It's in our genes. I can't go wrong with extra-large. Besides, if a shirt doesn't fit one, it'll fit another."

I waved to them as they rode up the escalator. My father held my mother by the elbow, his beige Members Only jacket folded neatly over his arm. They both looked so nervous, so frail, and my heart ached in letting them go alone.

Two weeks later

Querida hija:

How is Walter? I hope the two of you are doing well. I thought I'd write since when I call you it never quite seems like the right time, and I'm always so conscious of the money we're spending on these long distance calls. I want to tell you that your father and I have finally finished moving into my mother's house. We finally got water and gas, and the plumbing is finally working. I have to tell you that I miss my Frigidaire, and my Cuisinart, and my two Whirlpool machines. Can you believe that I have to get up at five every morning to wash your father's clothes with a washboard? I take the dirt out with the force of my arms. Sometimes I feel like I'm not up to this way of life, anymore.

Your father is getting along very well with your uncle, but he's starting to go out too much with him. He tells me that they're running errands together, but I know your uncle too well. I know that he's taking your father to those trashy bars to listen to music. Maybe you should talk to him.

Your mother

Walter finally came home last night, a week after not hearing from him. No phone call. No nothing. He confessed to me that he was having an affair with the office manager. She threatened to end the whole thing if he didn't leave me. The affair had been going on for almost a year. He said he felt like such a fool to put me through this. Could he make it up to me?

I didn't know if I was more angry than hurt. It wasn't like him to be so casual. My impulse was to let him come home and accept his apology as long as he promised to never see her again and to never talk about it again. But I restrained myself. I couldn't make things too easy, so I told him I needed to think about it. He could come home and sleep in my parents' room until I made up my mind and that we would have to go to couples counseling.

Two months later

Querida hija mía:

Your father's becoming a drunk. He goes out every night of the week with his buddies. I've disowned my brother for encouraging his behavior. Told him to not even think of ever stepping foot in the house again. The idiot had the nerve to tell me that the one who needed to leave was me. I told his wife that he spent the money we had lent him on a prostitute, and since then neither he nor your father are talking to me. Honestly, I don't care about him, but your own father siding with him—it hurts me very much. I feel like I'm suddenly all alone here. I'm asking the Virgin for patience, but I honestly don't know how much more I can bear.

Your mother

Couples counseling isn't what I thought it would be. I never realized how angry and bitter and just disappointed with life Walter has been. I feel like every time we go we're opening a can of worms I never knew existed. The counselor encourages him to talk about his adolescence. For Christ's sake, we keep spending session after session discussing why he couldn't get laid as a teenager. And it's costing us a hundred bucks an hour.

Last time, I felt like yelling to the goddamn counselor, "Can't you see he's having a midlife crisis!"

She's telling us to go on vacation, to take a cruise maybe, and that Walter should start taking antidepressants. Isn't that office whore enough of an antidepressant? Of course I kept my mouth shut the entire session and popped antacids all the way home.

Three months later

Querida hija:

I have exhausted all my prayers. I'm tired of asking for patience. I'm ready to come home, but your father has absolutely refused. He says he's staying for good—that he's prepared to die here. I told him that we've already paid for our plots in Los Angeles. He had the audacity to tell me that I'd be buried alone there and that it was just as well. Can you believe he said that? The neighbor told me about a spiritualist. They call her a spiritualist but the truth is she's a witch. I knew it the moment I walked into a storage room she has behind her patio and saw a room filled with a hundred or more candles all lit, right in the middle of the day. There were pictures of people all over the place, tattered black-and-white photos and Polaroids of babies, one of a woman in her wedding dress, another of a man in a military uniform. They were stuck to the wall, some on the floor. For a second I thought of turning back, but I didn't. I walked straight to her, and I had the nerve to tell her that I thought your father needed to learn a lesson, that he was acting like a macho pig, that after thirty-two years of marriage he was a pig, a swine, the lowest, dirtiest being on earth!

So guess what she did! She made my wish come true.

It happened at one of those disgusting, prostitute-infested bars he drinks at. They told me that your father was in the middle of one of his stories about how he made big money in Los Angeles, when he suddenly stopped and put his head on the table. His drinking buddies thought he had had a heart attack and insisted on walking him around the bar to see if he could recover his senses, but he pulled away from them, brought his arms to his chest, and started to move them in small circular movements—and then he started to snort. Everyone said that it was exactly like a snort. And when friends tried to grab him and calm him down, he let out a squeal! A tremendous squeal just like a three-hundred-pound pink pig your aunt has. One of the prostitutes got so scared she ran out of the bar screaming. They said that the bartender tried to shake your father out of it, but he couldn't. Then your father passed out. When he came to, he didn't remember a thing. In fact, he denied everything. He said everyone had gone mad. Your uncle got so scared that he threw up all night.

It has happened twice since then, and every time it seems to be getting worse. I think your father's really starting to get scared. At first, he didn't believe it, but now he seems lost in his thoughts most of the time. As for me, I've been going to Mass at least once a day. I still think this whole thing needs to go on a little more before I ask Doña Clemencia to undo the spell. She says that I can't wait too long because she'll lose control over it. But you know as well as I do that your father is a stubborn man. I'm going to wait another week or two.

Your mother

We've changed therapists. I don't think we were getting anywhere with the last one. Walter told me he wants to go on vacation alone. At first, I thought that was a good idea and then I find out that he's thinking of going on a two-week Princess Line cruise to the Carribbean. I pictured him on the cruiser with his lover, both of them lounging on the boat deck, basking in the sun, and I exploded with anger. And this time, I let it out! I said to him, "So help me God, if you buy the ticket, the marriage is over!"

I wish he'd grow a spine and just come out and say it and not waste all this time on therapy. The therapist said it didn't help to lose my temper the way I did, but it helped me.

The therapist insisted that I take up yoga, and so I started attending the yoga classes my gym offers, but I honestly don't really feel any different.

A telegram

Dearest niece:

Due to severe thunderstorms, the town has no electricity, maybe for the next two weeks, or longer. As your loving uncle, it is diffi-

`cult to express my sorrow and regret in informing you of your mother's incarceration. Please come and get her. Your loving uncle.`

My father has had my mother incarcerated. He had the town judge come to the house and formally accuse her of witchcraft. What's worse is she hasn't denied it. In my parents' remote hometown, this is a very serious offense. I don't know what my mother was thinking when she hired the witch to place a spell on my father. But my mother is a proud woman. She is not going to express remorse. I called my father and let him vent his frustrations. He told me that he's had a total of five episodes. The last one was a week ago. I pleaded with him to forgive Mom, but he wouldn't have it. If the town decided to leave her in there for ten years. So be it. Let her rot in jail, he told me.

I caught the red-eye to Morelia the same night I spoke to my father. What I was going to do there, I hadn't a clue. For one, I have no idea about the laws down there, and judging from my father's comment, there wasn't anything I could do. For another, my Spanish sucks. From what I've seen, Mexicans really hate it when Mexican Americans mutilate the language. They think you're stuck up or something. Or that you're not trying hard enough.

I arrived at four in the morning, their time, and as expected, it was thunder storming, no one spoke English, and I couldn't get a taxi to drive me all the way to Incarnacion. I'd have to take a taxi to Uruapan (for a hundred bucks) and then try to find another taxi to take me into town.

When I finally found a taxi (actually a four-wheel drive truck driven by the taxi driver's brother-in-law), the charge was an additional $120.00.

"What?" I said.

"Bad weather and twenty dollars extra for finding you this special taxi driver, señora." He was treating me like a moneyed *gringa*. I wished at the moment that my Spanish was good enough to tell him to go to hell, but of course, all I did was clam up and stare out the window.

When we started up the mountain, I felt light-headed and, at the same time, really into the moment. The sound of the strong motor, the winding roads, and the intense greens of the forest absorbed my attention.

When we reached the outskirts of Incarnacion, the taxi driver stopped. Where did I want to be dropped off? I didn't have a clue. It had all changed so much since I had been there as a child. We drove from house to house trying to pinpoint my mother's house. Finally, the taxi driver found someone who said that everyone was at the plaza. There was some kind of meeting.

We found a crowd of townspeople gathered at the church steps. From what I could gather, the meeting was supposed to be inside the church, but the priest had thrown them out.

The priest, a young man with thick glasses, stood at the church door. His wire-rimmed glasses slipped down his long nose as he yelled at the crowd. He was scolding them for being gossips and drama queens. "And there is no such thing as witchcraft. Now, go home." And he abruptly slammed the church door.

One of the men started laughing and another man joined him. "Drama queens," he repeated. The woman next to him, probably his wife, looked at him with repulsion.

"He has no right to treat us that way," she yelled. "And we all know what's happening is real. If he doesn't do something about it, we will."

There were groans. Another woman said, "We can prove it. How dare he?"

More groans.

Another woman said, "Let's take the vermin out, with or without the approval of the priest."

My heart sank. Five minutes later, I was ankle deep in mud trying to follow them up a narrow dirt road to a shack made of mud and wood with a rickety tin roof. The house was covered in bougainvillea vines that hid the entrance from the road. Three women went in, and I could hear yelling. I stood close to the entrance to see if I could hear my mother's voice. While the women stared at me suspiciously, they seemed too focused on the task at hand to do anything about it.

Eventually, a severely wrinkled old lady walked out. She was pretty, at least her face was. Her body was thin and quite hunched over with solid white hair made into one long braid. For all the commotion, she seemed quite calm.

She called them all a bunch of hypocrites. But they screamed back at her. One of the women had a broom in her hand. She looked fiercely at the old woman.

The old woman said to the crowd, "You've known what I do, your mothers knew what I did, and your grandmothers knew what I did. Fly, fly away, you pests." She jerked her hands in the air as though she was using a flyswatter. "Fly away, you pests, before I turn you into flies."

Several women took a step back, but the woman with the broom in her hand went back inside. I could hear her breaking things. Another woman went inside and took out all the candles that she could hold in her arms and threw them violently on the ground. Then the entire crowd went in and starting taking her things.

More women made their way to the corral and started to release the animals. The women chased the goats and the chickens out with their brooms, and the poor animals started falling from the top of an incline. I saw two poor goats fall a good hundred feet.

"Beasts, merciless beasts," the old woman yelled. "You'll all pay for this. I promise you."

Then two women came out with two huge pink pigs. One woman slapped the pig with her hand while the other woman attacked the pig with her broom. They were near the edge of the incline when one of the women shouted, "Stop!" The word pierced through the morning air. She called out to the other women, "What if one of these is my Pancho?"

The old woman said, "That pig is worth ten times that worthless *puto* husband of yours. He's in Mexico City with your whore sister. Everybody in town knows that. Even you know that, but you're too much of a coward to face the truth. Of course, that pig could be Pepe Sandoval, or maybe Nino Pérez." The women gasped, and the pigs turned around and went back into the corral.

Before I knew it, I was in my father's arms. He pulled me away, back down the hill, but I hesitated. "What if they try to hurt her?" I said to my father.

"She can take care of herself. This is not the first time this has happened. Doña Clemencia is over a hundred years old. Some say she has a contract with the devil. We need to help your mother. They will come after her next."

We found my mother crying in her bedroom. When my father heard about what had happened to Doña Clemencia, he went and had mother released from jail. She looked pale and thinner, and her eyes were puffy and bloodshot.

"If they hurt that old woman," she said, "I won't be able to forgive myself."

I gave her one of my sleeping pills and put her to bed at about noon. At about three that afternoon, the woman who had chased the goats off the cliff knocked on the door. "We want to talk to Concepción," she said.

"Concepción is my mother, what do you want?" I asked.

"We have business with her, ask her to come out and talk to us."

In those two or so hours that Mom had been asleep, I had made some makeshift weapons. I had a thick three-foot plank and my grandfather's machete ready if things got out of hand. My hands trembled in fear at the thought of using them.

"She's asleep," I said and was about to close the door.

"You don't look like a Rosales. You look white. People used to say you looked exactly like your mother, but you don't. We're not going away. Tell your mother to come out and talk to us or . . . "

My father grabbed the door and opened it. His arm was wrapped around my mother. My father walked with her out into the dirt road. "Do you have something to say to my wife? If you do, I'd like to hear it."

I wrapped the machete in a towel and slipped it under my raincoat. The size of the group of women had grown, and they looked as fierce as they had that morning.

"We heard you accused your wife of witchcraft. Is that true?"

"It is. So what? How does this concern you?"

"We're tired of this happening. We want you both to leave. We want you gone by tomorrow."

"Or what?" my father asked.

"Or we'll take matters into our own hands," one woman replied.

"I'll have you all know that I love my wife," my father said as he kissed my mother passionately on her forehead. "And whatever problems we have, they are our own. You prying bunch of vultures! We'll leave tomorrow."

I saw the look on my mother's face, a look of admiration and love and pride all at once. You'd think they had just renewed their vows.

As soon as the door was closed, we started packing. By midnight, everything was squared away. My mother took out the title of the house and signed it over to her brother. She called him over, and after so many years I was able to see my uncle again. He was, of course, quite pleased with the news. By early morning, we were in a taxi heading back to Morelia, and by that night we were back in Santa Monica fighting traffic on Sepulveda Boulevard. I took the long way home just so I could feel the cold ocean breeze against my face.

Two months later

The therapist told us to focus on the things we agreed on, which I thought was a really good idea. So we decided to focus on our Chihuahua, Frito. At first the idea seemed cute to me. Yes, he is my dog. And yes, we both do love him. But then, the conversation would get stuck on how Frito was depressed because we didn't walk him the way we used to, and his bowel movements weren't as regular as they could be, and how because he was getting up there in age, we needed to find a way to supplement his meals with calcium, and it just started to really piss me off. It wasn't cute anymore, and Walter was as distant as ever, and I am only thirty-two years old, and really, when you bottom-line it, I could still meet someone else and be happy. So that was it. It all seemed so clear to me, in a backward kind of way. I said in my deadpan voice, "Okay, so I think this marriage is over, and we won't be needing your services anymore. But thanks very much for trying." And I walked out, and if Walter walked out behind me, I wouldn't have known, because I wasn't looking back. The deal was done. And I didn't pop a single antacid pill on the way home.

About
The Chicano/Latino Literary Prize

THE CHICANO/LATINO LITERARY PRIZE was first awarded by the Department of Spanish and Portuguese at the University of California, Irvine during the 1974-1975 academic year. In the quarter-century that has followed, this annual competition has clearly demonstrated the wealth and vibrancy of Hispanic creative writing to be found in the United States. Among the prize winners have been—to name a few among many—such accomplished authors as Lucha Corpi, Graciela Limón, Cherríe L. Moraga, Carlos Morton, Gary Soto, and Helena María Viramontes. Specific literary forms are singled out for attention each year on a rotating basis, including the novel, the short-story collection, drama, and poetry; and first-, second-, and third-place prizes are awarded. For more information on the Chicano/Latino Literary Prize, please contact:

Contest Coordinator
Chicano/Latino Literary Contest
Department of Spanish and Portugese
University of California, Irvine
Irvine, California 92697